ROCK ME

Bodyguard Bad Boys

NEW YORK TIMES BESTSELLING AUTHOR

CARLY PHILLIPS

A pop star in danger.
Her reluctant bodyguard.
A past they can't deny.

Summer Michelle is on the verge of ultimate fame.

Ben Hollander has sworn off mixing business with pleasure.

But keeping his hands off of the sexy songstress is easier said than done and once the threat is neutralized, will she choose fame over love?

* * *

Chapter One

T HERE WERE BENEFITS to working for Alpha
Security, Ben Hollander thought, as he threw the
dart at the board in the company game room, nailing
the bull's-eye on the first try.

"Score," he muttered, smirking at Jared Wilson,
the colleague and friend he was playing with.

"Son of a bitch," the other man said. "At this rate
I'm going to be broke."

Ben shrugged. The guy should know better than to
wager with him. Ben was a crack shot at shooting
range practice they attended together on occasional
weekends.

"I don't know why you bother playing him," Ava
Talbott, the female bodyguard in their group, said.
"He kicks your ass every time."

"Because I've been practicing." Jared picked up a
dart, took aim, and hit right outside the coveted inner
circle, groaning at his near miss.

Ava snickered. "Obviously not enough." She snagged a fry off his plate and walked away. Jared didn't tear his gaze away from her ass as she left, heading for the table laden with food.

"Enough games. Time to meet up." The booming voice of their boss, Dan Wilson, echoed through the game room in the offices of Alpha Security.

The trio made their way to the conference room where Dan discussed cases and handed out assignments. They were missing the other members of the staff, Tate Shaw and Austin Rhodes, who were out on assignment.

They filed into the room where Dan had already taken up lead position at the head of the table. When not working, their boss was a big believer in blowing off steam during off hours, hence the game room with the pool table, dart board, and during lunch, an endless supply of eats. Located in the Whitestone area of the Bronx, there was no better bodyguard agency to work for in the tri-state area of New York, New Jersey, and Connecticut.

"Okay, kids, time for new assignments," Dan said.

Ben did his best to hold back a laugh. Dan considered all of his employees his children of sorts, although Jared was the only legitimate child of Dan's in the room. Still, he'd practically raised Ava from the time she'd been a lost teen whose mother was more interested in drugs than in her only kid. Dan had stepped into the role of parent, and though Jared and Ava had coexisted in the same house, the friction between them now wasn't that of siblings.

There was sexual tension there, pure and simple. Except it wasn't, because neither was willing to acknowledge it. At least so far.

"Sit," Dan directed, pointing to the chairs around the table.

All did as they were told, glancing up at the man who'd brought them into his business and paid them well. Standing before them wearing a pair of black slacks and a white button-down shirt, he was every inch the professional face of the security and body-guard firm.

Dan began speaking immediately, giving them an update on where each team member was or would be headed. "A lot of our assignments are status quo. Tate's in L.A. and the assignment was extended. Austin's tied up with the governor who's had threats leveled against him."

"What do you have for us?" Ava asked.

"Slow down, little girl," he said, using the affec-tionate endearment that always caused her to cringe— because she was a grown woman now. "I need you to meet with a new client. A mother who's worried her ex will come after her kid. She wants a female so her daughter isn't completely freaked out." He tossed a file Ava's way. All the preliminary information she needed would be included.

"Consider it done." Ava tucked her hair behind her ear and began to peruse the papers.

"Jared, you've been requested by a repeat client." He handed the folder to his son. "And that leaves Ben."

He rolled his shoulders, leaning his elbow on the table. "Let me have it, boss."

"You might not be so eager when you hear what it is, but keep in mind, we are out of options. Everyone's on another assignment." Dan eyed him with a healthy dose of an apology in his gaze followed by his tough-shit look.

The hair on the back of Ben's neck stood on end. "What's going on?"

"A little show-and-tell is in order for this assignment," Dan said, gesturing to the screen behind him. He pulled out his computer and tapped a few keys.

Up popped a photograph of Jade Glow, one of the world's most popular contemporary recording artists in the world. "Jade Glow needs an opening act for her fall tour and couldn't decide between two up-and-coming singers. Her solution? To give both women a chance to build their *star power* while she waits, watches audience reaction, and makes a decision."

Dan chose his words carefully. He always did. Which was why the words *star power* stood out like a beacon to Ben. Four years ago, he'd been a security guard on the set of the hit television show of the same name, where he'd met, fucked, and then proceeded to be fucked over by one of the show's up-and-coming stars.

He'd not only had an ongoing affair with one of the contestants, Summer Michelle, he'd violated his contract by doing so. Someone had turned him in and the producers had made it clear to him—the word had leaked from Summer herself. Ben had lost his job for consorting with the talent, while she'd gone on to tie for runner-up in the show. His current boss knew the whole sordid story, but he believed in second chances, and besides, Ben had come highly recommended from the firm he'd worked for prior to Dan's. He'd had to take a trial period while he earned his position and proved to his then-bosses he could be trusted to think smart on the job. Be a professional. Keep his dick in his pants. Not get taken in by a pretty face.

Ben's lesson had been learned the hard way.

"No. Fucking. Way." Another thing about Dan. He invited his people to speak their mind, which was why Ben had no problem expressing himself now. "If you are telling me I'm now bodyguard to Summer Michelle … that's a hell no."

Dan ran a hand over his cropped short salt-and-pepper hair. "I'm not finished with the explanation, although now that you've put together who's involved…" Dan hit a key on the laptop, and Summer's picture jumped onto the screen alongside a girl he remembered from the show as well, Tawny Renee.

Ben's visceral reaction to Summer's photo didn't bode well for this potential assignment. He hadn't seen Summer in years, but looking at her was like a punch to the gut and a kick start to his groin at the same time. The publicity photo accentuated her glossy black hair still long, still curling over her shoulders in a glorious silken wave. Her golden-brown eyes stared back at him while her pink lips were glossed in a pretty pout. And he distinctly remembered having those same lips wrapped around his dick while her tongue did her best to make him come.

Damn. How had fate landed her back in his lap?

Okay, bad choice of words, he thought, and cringed.

"You with me?" Dan asked.

Beside them, Jared and Ava were silent, no doubt either enjoying his discomfort or uncomfortable themselves with the situation Ben now found himself in.

"I'm listening," Ben muttered to Dan.

The older man nodded. "Vague threats have come

to Jade Glow's people regarding picking Summer for the opening act, so Orion Motors, the sponsor of her world tour, wants to hire protection for both women just to be safe."

"Are you giving me a choice of who I get to protect?" Ben asked. Neither option appealed. Tawny had been a spoiled brat with constant demands, but for some reason, Summer had liked the other girl. The two had been friends. Maybe that should have been Ben's first clue to steer clear of Summer Michelle.

"No. There's no choice for you. We're the best in the business, and Jade's people want us to look out for Summer since the threats focused solely on her. Unfortunately we have no other bodyguards to offer, at least for the moment, so they hired another firm for Tawny. You going to be okay?"

Since he didn't have a choice, he nodded.

"Good. Everything else you need to know about the case is in the file," Dan went on. "Her itinerary is in there as well, so you'll know where to meet up with her later today. She has a series of events lined up over the next month. You'll stick close."

"How close?" Ben asked warily. Some cases involved daytime surveillance only.

"Summer lives on the West Side in a one-bedroom walk-up. No doorman. No protection. So we're talking twenty-four-seven cover."

Of course they were. Because why should he catch a break?

They filed out of the room, Ben tense and really pissed at this latest assignment.

"Ben, wait up," Ava called out to him.

He wasn't in the mood to talk, but he slowed his step and waited for her to catch up with him.

"Hey," she said, placing a hand on his arm. "Are you okay?" Concern flashed in her gaze and expression.

"I'm fine."

She eyed him as if she wasn't quite sure she believed him. "And this assignment? I know it can't be easy for you. Dan knows it too. He's just cornered without anyone else to send in your place."

Ben nodded. "I get it. And I can handle it."

"I never said you couldn't. I just know you had feelings for this woman and—"

"And nothing. I've been burned and lived to tell the tale. I learned my lesson." Which Ava knew, since he'd opened up to her in a drunken moment when the team had all been available for a night out.

"Okay. Just know I'm here for you. Call if you need to talk or blow off steam." She squeezed his arm again and walked away. The people who worked for Dan were a tight-knit group, and Ben valued their friendship.

His job was important to him; it always had been. He took pride in protecting people, be it basic security as he'd done when he was younger and a few years after leaving the police force behind or now with Alpha Security. He wouldn't betray the people who meant so much to him.

As for Summer? He shook his head, the memory of that time still possessing the power to hurt him. In the tight world of the television show, the staff and talent had been together twenty-four seven. It had been easy for them to sneak away often, and although their time together had been brief, he'd believed they'd had a deeper connection. Something he'd honestly thought could turn into more over time, or else he never would have violated the terms of his contract. Not for a quick lay. Unfortunately she'd betrayed him for reasons he still couldn't fathom, and it burned in his gut because he should have known better.

Ben had seen his father humiliated and betrayed by his wife, yet Nate had taken his wife back the first time, only to be cuckolded again by Rita with the same man—Nate's longtime friend and partner. In the end, Nate Hollander had lost a lot more than his pride. He'd lost his business as well. He'd been a broken shell of a man after, that and Ben had sworn never to repeat his father's mistakes ... only to find himself screwed over by a woman.

Summer Michelle had been Ben's undoing four years ago, but he was determined not only to keep his distance but to make certain that he was the one calling the shots this time around.

SUMMER MICHELLE WAS living her dream, and how many people were able to say the same? This morning she'd rehearsed with the band the producers put together for her appearances, and now she was working with a stylist. She followed as the woman dragged her past rack after rack of clothing in the New York City showroom. She'd been instructed to choose a wardrobe for a variety of appearances she had coming up, from the opening of a restaurant to performing at a club to morning show appearances. All in conjunction with the competition to be the opening act for the world tour of Jade Glow, pop star extraordinaire.

Summer was a jeans-and-tee-shirt kind of woman, but if the dresses and elaborate designer clothing were any indication, that was about to change, and she had to admit she was extremely excited about the opportunity. She hadn't had any major appearances since the tour after the television show, *Star Power*, ended, and she'd been left to her own devices in choosing her clothing.

That had been four years ago, and now at twenty-six years old, she wasn't used to people telling her what to do or how to dress. But if she wanted the opportunity to open for Jade, she was going to have to learn to play the game.

Starting right now.

"So? Let's start with the colors that work best on you, yes?" Rose Lafoy, the stylist, asked.

"Black and white," Summer automatically said, glancing down at her black tee shirt, ripped jeans, and white sneakers.

Rose's eyes opened wide in horror. "No. Color. We want people to notice you. You need to stand out. You have a beautiful complexion, so let's bring out the gold in your eyes." She immediately began to pull warm colors, like reds, golds, and burgundy, and then she went on to explain Summer could also pull off bright blues, aquas, and deeper navy tones, as she layered clothing over her arm from the racks. "These are for daily wear. You can't run around the city like an average girl who blends in. Not if you want social media presence and coverage."

Other than Summer's voice, she *was* an average girl, but she had to stop thinking that way. She needed to remember to photograph the process, build her Instagram presence, her Snapchat stories, and a million other things she normally ignored so she could get lost in her head and create her music.

At the reminder, she pulled out her iPhone for a selfie with the clothes in the background, put on a playful pout, snapped, chose a filter, typed, "All in a day's work!" and hit share.

"Jessie, put these in the dressing room," Rose said to a harried-looking young girl, who hopped to do her bidding.

"Now for the club opening, what about this Chanel?" She chose a light gold beaded gown that appeared to have low cleavage and a high slit along one leg.

"Gorgeous!" Summer exclaimed, all the while wondering how she was going to hold her ample size C's in that skimpy dress.

"Good. And this Givenchy for the morning show appearance?" She lifted a bold yellow fitted dress that also had Summer pondering where she'd put the girls.

But the woman was a stylist and hopefully knew her business. "Let's try it!" She kept her excitement high despite her nerves.

She glanced at the time on her cell, wondering when the bodyguard she'd been assigned would appear. She'd been told he'd meet up with her at the stylist's studio. Thanks to some creepy, semi-threatening emails sent to Jade's PR firm, someone was fixated on the opening act. On Summer in particular, so the firm had hired protection for both her and

Tawny Renee, the other runner-up for the opportunity, just as a precaution.

Summer wasn't worried about the threat. There were plenty of crazy people out there who wrote nasty letters but didn't act out their fantasies. Still, in this day and age, you couldn't take a threat lightly, and Summer appreciated the security. Even if she thought it was unnecessary because she doubted she was the object of anyone's obsession.

"Come. Let's go to the sitting area," Rose said, breaking into her thoughts. "There's a private fitting room where you can try on the clothes, then come out and show me. Good? Good," she said without waiting for Summer to reply.

Summer followed her from the large room filled with racks of clothing into a spacious studio area, and then Summer went alone into the small back room to change. For the next thirty minutes, she dutifully performed the equivalent of a fashion show, twirling out into the lounge area to show Rose each outfit.

She donned skirts, dresses, shorts, and jeans, slipped on high-heeled Christian Louboutin heels—gorgeous shoes with red soles that she teetered in because she wore flip-flops in her normal life. Still, she smiled and preened her way out to where Rose and her assistant waited to appraise her, and after a while, the excitement of new clothes and Rose's elation were contagious. After accumulating a wardrobe of daywear for when the paparazzi caught her out getting Starbucks or traveling to and from the recording studio, it was time for the dressier items for the big events.

"Go. Start with the gold gown. I have to take a call," Rose called out to her. "I'll be right back."

Take your time, Summer thought. She could use a break from being constantly *on* for the bubbly French woman.

Summer had just stripped out of her last pair of designer-label jeans and sighed as she reached for the gorgeous gown. Knowing her bra wouldn't work, she pulled it off, unzipped the back, and stepped into the beaded, delicate dress.

Since she couldn't reach the zipper and needed Rose's help, she placed one hand on her hip, holding the material in place with the other hand, and pivoted toward the mirror for a first look. Her cleavage spilled out from the low V in front, but not in an inappropriate way. In a take-notice kind of way, for sure, but even she had to admit, she looked good, she thought, excited to show the stylist.

The fitting room was stuffy, so she headed out to wait for Rose in the bigger, airy sitting area. She was still falling out of the unzipped dress, but since it was just Rose and her assistant, her nearly exposed boobs didn't overly concern her. She'd be tucked in soon enough, and Rose would probably come running with Spanx to hold everything else in place.

She stepped into the main sitting area and stopped short, shocked to find a man standing there, leaning against the wall. Jet-black tousled hair, piercing blue eyes, strong jaw, and full lips she'd once experienced gliding over her body, bringing her to a fevered state of arousal, and kissing her like she'd never been kissed before. In their short time together, Ben Hollander had ruined her for all other men.

She'd never expected to see him again. Not since their affair while she was on *Star Power*, and his subsequent firing for fraternizing with the talent. He'd ignored her calls and disappeared from her life, never to be heard from again.

Until now. He stood in her dressing room, eyeing her with cool detachment, but as his gaze raked over her body and landed on her nearly exposed breasts, it darkened with a heat she recognized. Because she'd seen his eyes hooded with desire before.

Her nipples hardened, but she had no jacket to grab in order to cover herself, so she folded her arms across her chest and met his steady stare.

She finally found her voice. "What are you doing here?"

"I'm your new bodyguard. And if how easily I got in here is anything to go by, you desperately need one."

He'd worked security when she'd known him last. Now he was her bodyguard?

"Seriously? You're worried about how easily you got in here? I thought the PR people were just being cautious."

He narrowed his gaze. "I don't take anything about my job lightly. Not anymore," he said pointedly.

Direct hit and she winced at the overt reminder of their awkward past.

She never did know for sure how the producers found out about her relationship with Ben, but she if she had to guess, Tawny Renee had tattled. From the minute she and the other girl had met early on during filming of the show, Tawny had buddied up to her, and Summer had thought she was a friend. Until the night Tawny had turned on her, the end result being a girl fight video that had gone viral—Summer trying to get away, Tawny going after her for some imagined slight.

Only later had Summer discovered that Tawny staged the whole thing in an effort to build ratings. Just as she'd hoped, America had tuned in. And voted. She'd increased the rivalry that Summer would have preferred revolved around their voices, not their personalities. Unfortunately, prior to that incident, Summer had trusted her. Enough to fill her in on her time with Ben—because stupidly Summer had thought Tawny was a friend, just as she'd thought she had meant something to Ben, because he had sure meant something to her.

But, as she'd realized later on, the same girl who'd staged a cat fight would have no qualms about turning Summer in for violating the rules about sleeping with people working on set. No doubt she'd hoped they'd let Summer go due to the infraction, leaving Tawny as the front-runner on the show.

At the time, Summer had tried to get Ben's job back, begged the producers, explaining their affair was mutual. She'd even been willing to sacrifice herself, but they'd opted to make an example of Ben, firing him instead. Summer, they claimed, was too popular—a front-runner even before Tawny's staged event—to eliminate from the show.

She'd tried to call him and apologize. She'd texted her desire to talk and explain in person. He'd ignored her every attempt. From the tense set of his jaw, she doubted he'd care to hear her explanation even now.

He studied her intently, clearly letting her process the shock of seeing him and accepting his new position in her life.

She analyzed and came to one conclusion. "I really don't think you being my bodyguard is a good idea. You know, in light of our history."

"If I can handle it, I'm sure you can. Time has passed. We're both adults. It's business." His cold voice told her exactly where she stood.

"Fine." If he didn't mind being around her and protecting her, then she'd make the best of the situation and pretend his icy exterior didn't hurt her feelings at all.

Chapter Two

B EN TOOK ONE look at Summer and knew he was in trouble. She was a true mixture of ingénue and unknowing seductress. She'd folded her arms across her chest, but the action did little to conceal her ample cleavage and more to push up the swells of her breasts for his viewing pleasure.

He shifted positions. It was all he could do not to adjust his dick inside his pants.

"Oh, beautiful!" A woman with short-cropped dark hair walked in, clapping in delight. "I knew that dress was just perfect for your figure. Turn around. I'll zip you."

"Aren't you worried about who he is and what he's doing here?" Summer asked, pointing to Ben.

The woman shrugged. "I have clients with men in here all the time. It's nothing new. Now turn." She gestured and Summer spun around, revealing her sleek back and pale skin exposed thanks to the way her dress split down the center.

Ben swallowed hard. Hard being the word of the day now that he was around Summer again. He vividly recalled tracing that expanse of skin with his lips and tongue, how she'd trembled and moaned at his touch. Their time together had been short but potent, and he had to shake his head hard to dislodge the memories threatening to overtake him.

After finishing up with her new wardrobe, Summer headed back to the dressing room to change, reappearing in a pair of ripped jeans, black shirt, and white sneakers. Now she looked more like the girl he remembered, the eager-to-please, always-happy-to-perform woman who radiated happiness and sunshine. Fuck. He had to stop thinking like a guy who was whipped when it came to Summer and more like her security detail.

As he followed them into another room, he saw rack after rack of what had to be designer clothing and thanked his lucky stars he didn't have to sit through any more of the fashion show.

"Thank you so much for today," Summer said to the stylist, whose name he'd learned was Rose. "I just love the clothes and can't wait to wear them." She gestured to the huge pile she'd accumulated.

"What's next on the agenda, princess?" he asked, an unplanned sarcastic tone to his voice to help offset his attraction to her. One that was still there and not something he welcomed.

She spun toward him, her gaze narrowed. "Excuse me?"

"Isn't that what you are? A pop princess?"

Her lips pursed in annoyance. "Except coming from you, it sounds more like an insult than a compliment."

And he, of all people, knew how much her music career meant to her. How much she'd sacrificed, including friends and a normal childhood. Because during the time they'd spent together, she'd confided so much to him, including her hopes and dreams. He was a dick for belittling them now just because she made him feel things he didn't like or want to experience again.

"I want a new bodyguard. Someone I trust." She hit back where it would hurt him the most, because he'd confided in her too and he prided himself on a job well done. On being someone trustworthy and reliable.

And this verbal sparring was getting them nowhere, so he held up his hands in surrender. "Stop. What I said was uncalled for. We're both professionals. We can handle this arrangement for as long as is necessary. No more low blows."

She swallowed hard, the soft line of her throat

moving up and down. He wanted to trace the silken skin with his tongue, bite down until he marked her and she moaned like he knew she would. Those sounds she used to make in the back of her throat when he was deep inside her still haunted him.

"Fine," she said, breaking into his irreverent daydreams before he could go further, before his body could react to the thoughts he couldn't control in his brain.

At least she'd acquiesced easier than he'd expected. "So what is next on your agenda?" he asked in a rough voice.

She rubbed her bare arm with one hand. Her nails were long and painted a light blue.

"Errands and then home. I have an early appearance on *The Morning Show*. It's a short interview and then I'm performing."

"Indoors or out?" he asked, already assessing the situation and risk.

"Out."

He blew out a sharp breath. He'd just have to stick close to the stage. "Fine. When we get back to your place, I need to see your most recent itinerary. Make sure nothing's changed compared to what was given to me."

She nodded in agreement. "Okay. And you'll come by in the morning and go with me to the studio?"

He couldn't stop the slow grin from lifting the corners of his mouth. "Nope. I'll be spending the night, so please tell me you've got a decent-sized couch?"

She blinked, and those big doe eyes looked at him as if surely he'd lost his mind. "Why would you need to stay over? I'm perfectly safe locked in my apartment until you come to get me."

He cocked an eyebrow. "In your walk-up apartment with no doorman or alarm? Is that really your definition of perfectly safe?"

She opened her mouth to argue, then shut it again, obviously realizing she really couldn't fight him. The fact was, this was his business and he knew it better than she did.

She blew out a long breath. "You're in luck," she muttered, somewhat ungraciously. "I have a pullout sofa so that big body of yours won't have to curl up on a too-short couch."

He smirked, realizing he was enjoying watching her squirm. "I can't wait."

Ben had taken the subway to get to Summer's appointment because he'd been told she had car service provided by Jade Glow during the time of the so-called competition. From the stylist's, a waiting car drove them to Summer's. Ben was grateful he didn't have to deal with keeping her safe in subways loaded with people or taxi cabs with random drivers. Rose had sent her home with tomorrow's clothes and promised to deliver everything else. Without a door-man, Summer instructed Rose to leave everything with the super in her building.

When they arrived, Ben's suspicions about her apartment were confirmed. The place was a security nightmare. Anyone could come into the building just by following close behind someone heading in. Her lock wasn't any more secure, something he'd take care of right away by getting one of his company's trusted locksmiths to put a secure Medeco lock and deadbolt on the door.

"Be it ever so humble," she said, opening the door and letting him inside first.

He looked around her home, taking in the bright colors and homey atmosphere. A white canvas sofa was covered in red and yellow pillows and there was a black-and-white area rug beneath the cocktail table, which he assumed would move easily so he could open the bed hidden inside. The kitchen was a tiny, narrow room, the eating area a small table at the end of the entryway and just outside the kitchen. A pass-through window opened to the family room. There was nothing pretentious about how she lived.

He placed his bag down beside the sofa.

"The bathroom is through there," she said, pointing to the door beside her bedroom, a short couple of steps away from where he'd be sleeping, something he wouldn't think about until he absolutely had to.

"I think we'll manage just fine," he said, wishing he were as confident as he sounded.

But the last thing he was ready to do was spend God knew how many nights in this small apartment, surrounded by the fragrant scent of wildflowers he associated with Summer.

★　★　★

SUMMER COULDN'T SLEEP. Dinner, which she'd prepared for them both, consisted of whole wheat bow tie pasta with fresh vegetables and tomato sauce, and lackluster conversation. In the background, a locksmith had changed her locks and secured her home, but Ben wouldn't have been chatty even without the worker there. There seemed to be a definite tension between them leftover from their time together and the past, and he seemed determined to do his job with no other real conversation between them. So she gave him what he wanted and turned in early to her room for bed. But first she'd helped him open the pullout sofa and made up the bed for him to sleep.

Her apartment had one bathroom outside the bedroom, and so she waited until she heard him come out before heading in to wash up and change into a pair of light blue sleep shorts and a matching tee shirt, making sure she didn't glance his way when she exited. The last thing she wanted to do was catch him shirtless, because the guy had a freaking fantastic chest. All hard muscle and lean abs that had felt so amazing against her hands, her belly, her entire body when they came together.

With a groan, she shook her head of those thoughts or else she'd never be able to get to sleep tonight. Once back in her room, she noticed her phone had a text from her best friend, Ivy Jameson. A web designer, she worked from home and had been busy on deadline or else she'd have been all over coming with Summer to her stylist appointment earlier today.

Ivy: *So? Loaded with designer duds?*

Summer typed in her reply. *You have no idea. Gorgeous stuff.*

Ivy: *Bodyguard show up yet?*

She'd told Ivy about the plan to provide her with security.

She replied immediately. *Again, you have no idea.*

Oh, Ivy knew all about Summer's past. They'd had too many girls' nights for them not to know all about each other. But nobody could have anticipated Summer's new bodyguard being *the* man from her past.

Ivy: *Is he hot man candy?*

Summer: *Yes.*

And that one word did not accurately capture all that was Ben Hollander. It wasn't just his exceptional good looks, it was his presence, made even stronger by that hot body. Muscles bulged from beneath the tee shirt and the weapon she knew he carried that was there to keep her safe. And even though he was obviously still angry at her, that brooding thing was sexy, too. She was so screwed, and not necessarily in a good way.

Ivy: *One-word answer? What aren't you telling me?*

Just that he could make her panties melt with one searing look.

Summer: *It's Ben. And before you ask, yes, that Ben.*

Ivy: *OMG. Second chances and hot summer sex?*

She wished. *He's still angry and bitter. He's not speaking to me much beyond doing his job.*

Ivy: *His job is to guard your body. Show it off and you'll be fine.*

She brushed a strand of hair off her face and lowered herself onto the bed. If only the solution to her and Ben were that easy. They had a lot of unfinished business between them that only talking about would help, but he didn't seem like he was in the mood to listen.

She turned her attention back to her friend and typed. *He's staying here as part of the security detail.*

Ivy: *Perfect. Use the time to make things right. You know you want to. Then see what happens between you.*

She replied, *We'll see... XO,* and put her phone on the nightstand.

She thought about what Ivy said, at least about making things right. He hadn't wanted to take her calls after he was fired, but they had forced proximity now. He'd have to talk to her if she pushed the issue. She didn't know if she could melt his icy exterior, but she could ease her conscience. Not that she'd been at fault, but he obviously thought she was. And that bothered her.

She climbed into bed and tried to sleep, but thoughts of the man in the other room kept her tossing and turning. An hour later, with no sleep, she decided maybe a cup of hot tea would help.

She walked out of her room, surprised to find a

small light on and Ben sitting upright in the bed. "Hey. What are you doing up?" she asked.

"Couldn't sleep. You?"

"Same. I thought I'd make myself a cup of tea. Can I get you some?"

"No thanks."

She headed for her kitchen and turned on the stove to boil water, then she took a mug from the cabinet, her thoughts on what Ivy had said.

Make things right.

Talk to him.

Maybe it was time.

★ ★ ★

BEN HAD BEEN tossing and turning when Summer walked out of her room. It wasn't the bed that was the problem. He'd slept in more awkward accommodations on assignment. It was the woman in the next room and how uncomfortable things were between them. Not to mention the fact that he found her as desirable now as he had then, more so because she'd developed an air of confidence as she'd matured, and he found it fucking sexy.

She'd turned on the light in the kitchen, and one glimpse through the pass-through window revealed her ample, braless breasts, visible through the thin cotton. He pressed a hand against his aching dick.

"I called you, you know. More than once," she said as she went through the preparations of making her tea, turning on the stove top and putting a bag in a mug.

He didn't pretend not to know what she was referring to. He'd seen her calls. Had ignored them. He wasn't proud of it, but he'd been humiliated by the experience and furious with himself for knowingly putting himself in a position to be fired.

He didn't want to have the conversation now, but she deserved an answer. "I wasn't in a good mental place to take your call or talk about what happened."

She walked out of the kitchen and sat on the edge of the bed. "I'm sorry." She looked down at her hands, which were clasped tightly together. "You were angry and you had a right to be, but I need you to know something. I had nothing to do with the producers finding out about us. I have my suspicions who snitched, but that doesn't matter now."

She lifted her head, raised her shoulders, and met his gaze. "What matters is you knowing that I begged them not to fire you. I told them what happened between us was mutual. I even said that I seduced you and offered to leave the show myself."

She surprised him and not much did these days. "It was a long time ago and I learned a valuable lesson. It's fine," he said in a gruff voice. But it wasn't good enough and he knew it. "I could have handled it better." He shrugged. "Answered your calls."

"Can we be more … civil to each other now?" she asked.

He wasn't sure he could handle civil with her and not cross that line again. Especially with the attraction between them still hot as ever.

"Distance lets me do my job."

She placed a hand on his foot, covered by a blanket … which he felt all the way to his cock. "I'll take that as a yes," she said with a cheeky grin, squeezing his toes once before the teakettle began to whistle.

She rose to shut off the stove top, and he couldn't tear his gaze away from the sway of her hips or the curve of her ass in those shorts. He watched her pour the water into her mug before adding some milk and sugar, her movements lighter and happier than they had been before, lightening the heaviness that had been in his chest.

He refused to consider why.

Chapter Three

SUMMER WOKE UP, a bundle of nerves in her stomach. Today was her first national appearance since her days on *Star Power*, and so much was on the line. This was the break she'd been waiting for her entire life. If she lost out on the opportunity to open for Jade Glow, she would have to reevaluate everything she'd worked and strived for since she was a little girl.

She'd been on *Star Power* when she was twenty-two, and now she was twenty-six years old, doing voice-overs and making a very nice living but not living her dream or doing something she was passionate about. She pushed off the thoughts of the crossroads she'd be at if this opportunity fell through and focused on today's performance. *The Morning Show* would do an interview with both her and Tawny, then each of them would sing individually. She had a song she'd written and was excited to perform live. Her pre-audience nerves always disappeared once the music took over her entire being.

She blew out a deep breath and readied herself in her bedroom, snapping selfies and posting pre-appearance photos on her various social media sites. She'd undergone many hair and makeup lessons in an effort to save herself money in the days before she'd begun doing voice-overs, and she had no problem pulling herself together. She knew *The Morning Show* had makeup artists who would make sure she was television ready before she went live.

She made herself a protein shake while Ben showered, and she kept her mind off the hot naked man a room away, whose rock-hard body she vividly remembered and she was dying to see again.

Instead she focused on the song she was going to sing. Which wasn't easy when the bathroom door opened and he stepped out with a towel wrapped around his waist, his hair damp from the shower, his muscles flexing, his tanned skin glowing.

She paused with her drink halfway to her mouth and swallowed over the sudden arousal pulsing through her body. "Umm … good morning."

"I thought you were in your room," he said in a gruff voice.

"I figured I needed something in my stomach so I don't pass out in front of an audience." She lifted her glass with her breakfast blended inside.

"You'll be fine. The stage is definitely a place where you shine." He looked shocked he'd complimented her before schooling his expression into his usual bland look.

She didn't care that his words had slipped out. He'd said them and she beamed at his compliment. "You really believe that?"

"Yeah. I do. I remember watching you from the side of the stage on *Star Power*. You captivated your audience and had them in the palm of your hand. You've got this," he said in a reassuring tone. "And now I need to get dressed if we're going to make sure you arrive at the studio on time."

He turned away from her, exposing the firm lines of his back and the flex of muscles as he bent down to pull clothing from his duffel bag.

She regretfully dragged her gaze away and told herself to stop wishing she could run her hands over his taut skin and feel those muscles flex beneath her fingertips or her lips. After one last lingering glance, she headed back into her bedroom while he dressed.

Rose had sent her home with an aqua jeweled tank top and black spandex, which she changed into, leaving her hair down and curled. Her shoes were her favorite performing shoes, a pair of black patent booties with a chunky but high heel she had no trouble strutting around on stage in. She wasn't about to risk wearing the pair Rose had sent her home with, which would no doubt result in an embarrassing tumble without practice wearing them.

She stepped out of her bedroom to find the couch put back together and Ben sitting on the sofa, drinking a cup of coffee. His gaze swung to hers, his light blue eyes opening wide at the sight of her, darkening with heat as they took in her whole outfit.

Her body shocked with what felt like an electric current, and her nipples puckered tight at the sexual need and admiration in his gaze.

"Like what you see?" She couldn't help but tease him like she had in the old days, when things were easy and fun between them.

"Behave," he said in a gruff voice.

She refused to be deterred, having decided she was going to win him over by sheer force of will and a perpetual good mood. "You can say it. It won't kill you. *Summer, you look good.*"

An unwilling half smile pulled at his lips. "Summer, you know damn well you look good," he said, rising from his seat.

It was a small concession, but it gave her intense pleasure to hear his admission. Besides, the outline of his erection tenting his pants was a blatant stamp of approval on her appearance.

"Now let's get going before you're late."

Too quickly, they'd made the trip by car to the studio uptown. A greeter met them at the entrance and escorted them to the Green Room. Someone came by immediately to touch up her makeup, getting rid of any shine, then she was instructed to remain there and wait to be called.

Tawny was there as well, along with her entourage, a man Summer assumed was her bodyguard, and her agent, Michael Gold, a blond man in his mid-forties with a reputation as both a flirt and a shark in the business. As a matter of fact, it was through Tawny's agent that Summer had found her own representation, Anna Davis. He'd been happy to recommend someone at his agency at the time Summer had been looking.

Michael stood extremely close to Tawny but Summer merely shrugged. He didn't understand the meaning of personal space with her, either. Anna wasn't here but there was no reason for her to be. Michael was a different kind of agent. Summer didn't require the amount of handholding that Tawny did.

Also circling Tawny were her friends, who fawned over her … and her parents. The sight made Summer's stomach clench with the familiar sadness that her parents weren't here, too. They were traveling in Europe, leaving Summer to handle her career. Their itinerary was fluid, and she expected a call when they were back in South Carolina, where they'd bought a retirement home.

Things hadn't been the same between them since she essentially fired them as her manager and agents soon after she'd been runner-up in *Star Power*. Her reasons had been valid. She'd lost a key booking because they'd pushed too hard at the wrong time, and she knew then she'd needed professionals. All the people involved with the show had told her so. Unfortunately she'd created a rift between them she'd never intended.

Anna was solid and in her corner, a good professional fit, but she missed the close-knit family feeling she'd had when her parents traveled with her. But her mother and father couldn't differentiate between being her parents and controlling her career, so they'd agreed it was better for them not to tag along. And though Ivy showed up when she could, her presence was dependent on whether or not she had urgent deadlines for her website business.

Summer turned her gaze away from Tawny and her people, rubbing a hand over her stomach, willing away both her unwanted emotions and her performance nerves.

"Summer!" Michael called as he made his way over to her. "How are you?" He came up close, into her personal space.

She immediately stepped back, which made Ben slip in beside her, his protective instincts coming to the surface.

"This is Michael Gold, Tawny's agent," she said to Ben. "Michael, this is my bodyguard, Ben Hollander."

The men shook hands, and Summer couldn't get over how different they were in both build and stature. Michael wasn't a bad-looking man, but he wasn't Summer's type and he was small compared to Ben's more muscular frame.

And where Ben was secure in himself, Michael was flashy in his designer suits and the gold Rolex he displayed by constantly rolling his dress shirt sleeves to put it on full display. Added to that, he drove a vintage Rolls Royce and made sure everyone knew it. But he was a top agent, and that's all that mattered from a client's perspective.

"Are you ready?" Michael asked her with a wink. "Stiff competition." He gestured toward Tawny.

"I can handle it," she assured him.

"Good. I like a good competition." He walked away, onward to do his thing.

Ben scowled after him. "I don't like him," he muttered.

"He's pompous but harmless."

"So just to go over today's scheduling," the producer of the show said, interrupting them. "You'll be interviewed and perform immediately after. Tawny is up first. Break a leg," he said, clasping her forearm before walking away, pulling out his phone as he left the room.

She blew out a disappointed breath.

"What's wrong?" Ben asked, perceptive to her sudden mood shift.

"Going second means I can't set the bar high. I have to surpass whatever bar Tawny sets." She rolled her shoulders, pulling in a deep breath and willing herself to relax. "It'll be fine," she said, trying to convince herself.

Because Tawny was many things Summer didn't like, but she was definitely talented, and Summer would have much rather put the pressure on *her* than vice versa.

Before Ben could reply, a woman with a clipboard strode into the room. "Tawny, you're up."

Tawny turned and headed for the door, stopping by Summer. Her blonde curls bounced around her face, and she pasted on her patented fake smile.

"Hi, Summer."

"Tawny."

The other woman's gaze shifted to Ben. "Well, I'll be damned. Ben Hollander. That's who they assigned as your bodyguard?" She shook her head in disbelief.

"I'd say it's a pleasure but I'd be lying," Ben said.

"Right. Because Summer thinks I'm the one who outed your affair."

Ben raised an eyebrow. He had no idea what Summer believed because she'd never shared her opinion with him, thinking the hows and whys no longer mattered. Tawny had a long memory and she liked to stir up trouble.

"Did you?" Ben asked.

"You'll never know," she said and turned to Summer, her gaze raking her over from head to toe. "Nice outfit. You think biker chic will appeal to America?" she asked with disdain.

The friends behind her giggled at the not-too-subtle dig. Tawny had opted for a softer lacey look, her entire outer appearance at odds with the hard, ambitious girl on the inside.

"I think America will appreciate good music," Summer said, never quite having the right comeback for the other woman's bitchiness.

"Whatever you say. I'm going to kick ass." She flipped her hair and strode off.

Summer glanced at Ben, who'd been holding up the wall beside Summer, taking in everyone and everything around him. "She's something else," Summer murmured.

"She's a bitch," Ben said.

Ever since the staged cat fight at *Star Power*, Tawny had done little to hide her desire to get ahead or her mean-girl side. Summer figured it had been her own naiveté—and the fact that she'd rarely had exposure to cliques and girls with attitude because she'd been homeschooled and had been too busy performing— that had prevented her from seeing Tawny for who she was the first time they'd met.

Live and learn.

Ben pushed himself off the wall and, towering over Summer, grasped her shoulders. "This is what you do best. Your strength is performing, and you will be the one who kicks ass." He met her gaze and winked at her, a sparkle in his usually intense eyes, his not-so-subtle way of reinforcing that no matter what had happened between them, he believed in her talent.

At this moment in time, with a morning show audience awaiting her, she'd take his confidence and tuck it away inside her.

★   ★   ★

ON THE SCREEN in the Green Room, Ben watched with Summer as Tawny rocked her moment on TV. As much as he wanted to reassure Summer that she didn't have a big shadow to live up to, that would be a lie. He still knew she could nail her performance and make a huge impression.

He'd prefer to do his job and keep his distance, but it was hard when she didn't have anyone in her corner except for him. He hadn't missed the longing in her expression when she'd seen Tawny's entourage, and he wondered why her parents weren't here to support their daughter. They'd barely left her alone back during the *Star Power* days. Although he'd been curious enough to ask, he knew she needed to be focused on her upcoming stage time, and he didn't want to upset her even more.

Now, he stood backstage, keeping an eye out for anything amiss as Summer talked to *The Morning Show* host, holding her own, joking and enjoying herself on stage. By virtue of her real personality, she was more natural and likeable than Tawny. Just as Ben had assured her, the minute she stepped into the limelight, she shone. She brought people into her warmth—even him, and he knew remaining detached would be damned difficult.

She took her place on stage as the band began to play. Ben couldn't tear his gaze from the outline of her curvy body in that sexy outfit she wore, the tank top that accentuated her full breasts, and skintight black leggings that encased her toned calves and thighs. And he'd felt those legs wrapped around his waist, ankles crossed at his back as she urged him to fuck her harder. Okay, maybe she hadn't used that word, but the impact of her sexy groans and the clasp of her body as she'd pulled him tighter had the same impact. He shifted his position, glad he was hidden in the shadows to do his job.

She began to sing, and he was transported back to the first time he'd heard her sultry voice. He'd been impacted then and she was even better now. It was difficult for him to maintain the focus he needed on the people around her when all he wanted to do was get lost in the beautiful strains of her voice.

Suddenly her eyes opened wide, a panic-stricken look on her face. He scanned both the crowd and the stage, but on his end, everything was fine. One hand on his holstered weapon ... just in case, he held himself in place despite the overwhelming urge to pull her off the stage and find out what was wrong.

She tapped the earpiece and frowned as the crowd began to boo.

SUMMER'S EARPIECE WAS dead. One minute she'd begun her performance, her band's music in her ear, clear and on time, and out of the blue, she heard nothing but the roar of the crowd around her, the muffled sound of the instruments coming in with echoes and distortion from the speakers. And then her audience began to react and they weren't happy. They weren't interested in technological glitches and neither was she. She knew opportunity when she saw it, and she wasn't about to lose this one.

She turned to the band and made a motion with her hand, indicating they should stop playing. Then she tossed the earpiece out of her ear, positioned the microphone in front of her, and began to sing. A capella. Without instrumental accompaniment.

The crowd quieted down and listened, and Summer continued, picking up the beat until the audience was clapping and singing along with her. Her adrenaline, which had been born of fear and panic, turned to a rush of excitement and joy. She worked her way through the song, bending down in order to touch hands with the people in the front row enjoying the show. She'd won them over, and the relief coursing through her was huge.

She finished the song to a rousing round of applause, which she graciously accepted before heading to the right side of the stage, where Ben waited. Her heart was pounding hard in her chest, the thunderous live applause still echoing around her, and the rush of success and pride in overcoming what could have been a disaster had her soaring.

"Did you see that?" she asked Ben. "My earpiece went dead and I nailed it anyway!"

"You totally did," he said, a huge grin on his face

that let her know he understood what a big moment this was.

She squealed in excitement and threw her arms around his neck, needing to share her exhilaration. Their gazes met and locked, the air around them suddenly crackling with tension and sexual need even Ben couldn't deny.

She knew what she wanted, knew there was no better time to go about it. Her gaze fell to his mouth and she pressed her lips against his. He jerked in surprise, then groaned, thrust his hand beneath her hair, holding her against him as he slid his tongue past the seam of her lips and kissed her back.

He might think he wanted to keep his distance, but his body was demanding they get close, his mouth gliding back and forth over hers, razor stubble bristling her cheeks in a sweet burn, and his tongue delved deep. Against her stomach, she felt the hard press of his erection, causing desire to sweep over her in waves.

No wonder she hadn't found a guy she wanted to keep in her life. No one could live up to Ben.

He kissed like he wanted to possess her.

Own her.

Keep her.

"Summer! Summer, what happened?" Her agent's voice penetrated the delicious fog that had enveloped her and Ben. She ignored her for a few more blissful seconds, taking in the feel of Ben's lips, his tongue tangled with hers.

"Summer!"

"Anna!" She straightened and forced herself away from Ben and faced her agent. "I didn't realize you'd be here."

"I wanted to support you! What happened?" she asked, concerned.

"Yes, what happened?" Michael walked up beside her, joining their small group.

Ben straightened his shoulders and took a step back, letting her focus on her professional life. But a glance at his steely gaze and her stomach churned uncomfortably at the cool look in his eyes, telling her in no uncertain terms that he regretted that lapse in his precious self-control.

She frowned before turning to her agent, who she knew expected an explanation. "The earpiece went dead. I had no choice but to improvise."

A flash of distress crossed Anna's face. "But you stepped up and did great! Everyone's talking about how you pulled out a win. Congratulations." Her agent touched her shoulder in support. "Isn't she a star?" she said to Michael.

He smiled back, but as he was pulling for Tawny, his gaze was rather cool. Speaking of Tawny, she glared at Summer from her corner of the backstage area. No *great job* would be forthcoming from her rival.

"We are so sorry!" The producer of *The Morning Show* came rushing over to Summer. "I don't know what happened. The equipment worked fine for Tawny but you were amazing. Social media is going crazy for your performance!" The woman smiled and rushed off to handle another crisis.

"Summer, I'll talk to you later," Anna said and headed away as well.

Summer turned to Ben, wanting to address the moment despite the fact that the adrenaline pressing at them had passed. He might regret what had happened between them, but she didn't. Not at all.

"Can we go?" he asked, all business.

"Umm, sure."

He grasped her elbow in a professional hold and led her past the backstage crowds.

Gone was the hot-blooded man in whose arms she'd lost herself for a few glorious seconds, and back was the cool, calm, unaffected bodyguard. He was right by her side, but the distance he placed between them might as well have been miles. If she thought she had broken through his reserve, she'd been sadly mistaken and was definitely disappointed.

BACK AT HER apartment, Summer changed into a pair

of leggings and an oversized tee shirt and kept herself busy while waiting for Ivy, who was coming over in a little while to hang out. She spent time on the phone with Anna arranging voice-over work with companies who had contacted her agent with interest, and puttered around the apartment, watering her plants and straightening up. She deliberately ignored the man sitting on the sofa making himself at home.

If he'd acknowledged the kiss or discussed the intimate moment between them, then she'd be more willing to move forward like two adults. He had a job to do, to protect her, and she didn't want to make it more difficult. But the fact that he was deliberately pretending like that kiss hadn't happened pissed her off and hurt her feelings. She just hadn't decided how to handle him yet.

Instead of dealing with him, she headed for the kitchen, took out two glasses, and poured herself some wine, setting one aside for Ivy. She settled into a chair at the kitchen table, scrolling through her laptop, checking her various social media sites for mentions of today's performance.

A YouTube video had already gone viral, and a photo with contrasting shots of her panicked face when she realized the earpiece was dead and her triumphant hand pump at the end when she'd nailed her performance had hit the entertainment blogs.

She'd been hailed a success, but all in all, it had been a long day.

A knock sounded at the door, and she jumped up to let her friend in. Ben beat her to it, his big body blocking the entire entrance. "Who's there?" he asked in a rough voice.

"It's my friend Ivy." She tried moving him over, but he was like a brick wall.

"Ivy Jameson," a familiar female voice replied from the other side of the door.

"You see?"

Ben unlocked the door and opened it partway. "ID please."

"That's ridiculous. I can vouch for her." Summer grasped his forearm, shocked by the hard muscles she encountered and the jolt that went through her system at the innocent touch.

He stiffened, obviously affected, too.

She pulled her arm back and curled her fingers into a fist.

Ivy slipped her license to Ben.

He studied it and handed it back. "And you're alone?" he asked.

"Yes. One hundred percent I'm here by myself," Ivy said.

Ben put a hand on his weapon and waited as Ivy slipped inside. "Hi. Ivy Jameson. Best friend," she said, extending her hand to Ben.

"Ben Hollander. Bodyguard." He shook her hand and glanced at her with the passing interest of a man doing his job and studying the newest visitor. Not that of a man captivated by the woman in front of him, which was curious because with her blonde hair, light brown eyes, and slender figure, Ivy turned most men's heads.

Ben stepped to the door and turned the deadbolt once more, locking them all inside before heading back to his position on the sofa in front of the TV.

Ivy hooked her arm with Summer's, and they walked toward the kitchen. "So that's your hot ex?"

One thing about Ivy was her overly loud personality. Even in this small setting, her voice carried, and Summer had no doubt Ben had heard over the sounds of the television.

"Shh." Summer's cheeks heated, and to shut her friend up, she handed Ivy her glass. "Here. Take a drink."

"I'd love one. Tell me all about today! I saw you on TV. I was so worried, but you were amazing, singing without your band and getting the audience to eat out of your hand. I was cheering out loud."

Her words and tone held a pride Summer needed to hear from her friend. Someone close to her who understood how hard she'd worked for the opportunity she had and how important every appearance was toward her goal. She'd hoped to hear from her mother or father, even from far away they knew her schedule, but so far there'd been no word.

She took a long sip of her wine, finishing the glass and pouring another.

"Whoa. Let me catch up!" Ivy laughed and took a big drink of her own.

"I'm so glad you're here," Summer said, pulling her friend into a hug. "Thank you for coming over."

"My best friend is on *The Morning Show* and kills it. Where else would I be but here to celebrate?" Ivy tapped her glass against Summer's.

For the next couple of hours, they talked and drank, and when the pizza Ben had ordered arrived, they shared that as well and drank some more.

Ben maintained his seat on the couch, which continued to aggravate her, his aloof manner driving her to distraction. While she couldn't get that kiss out of her mind, he seemed to have put it behind him, and easily at that.

Pouting and tipsy, she leaned closer to Ivy, who had just finished regaling Summer with a story about her latest date, an online site disaster of a matchup.

"I kissed Ben after the show today," Summer whispered.

Her friend started to reply, and Summer placed a

hand over her mouth before Ivy could shout something Summer didn't want Ben to hear. "He hasn't mentioned it since," she said just as softly.

"He's a tough one." Ivy glanced over at Ben. "I think the fact that you're both under one roof is going to make things escalate sooner rather than later."

"I hope so," she said and poured another glass of wine for fortification.

Chapter Four

BEN TOLD HIMSELF that the earlier kiss had been the result of Summer's adrenaline rush and nothing more. He wasn't sure he believed it, not given how quickly it had escalated, how good her lush body felt in his arms, and how hard he was for her even now, hours later. But he had no choice but to push forward and do his job, and that meant pretending the kiss had never happened. Which wasn't easy when he was in Summer's orbit, surrounded by her soft scent and the driving need he had to do more than just kiss her.

The women were talking to each other in the small kitchen area. Despite having the television on, he'd just heard the story of Ivy and her last date, something he wished he could un-hear.

"You'll never guess who I ran into at Starbucks," Ivy said, her voice louder with each successive glass of wine.

"Who?"

"Your ex, Ryan."

"Really? How does he look?" Summer asked.

If he was an ex, why did Summer care how this Ryan guy looked? he thought with an irritable frown.

"His hair grew and he has a beard. He looked good."

"Too bad he sucked in bed," Summer said, ending that sentence on a giggle that had to be the result of too much wine.

Jesus. The last vision he wanted was one of Summer naked and in bed with some guy named Ryan. Or any guy, for that matter, whether or not he was bad in the sack. Ben wished he had the luxury of drinking like the women were, but he didn't indulge while on the job.

"He did say to tell you he'd like to hear from you again."

Despite himself, Ben cocked his head their way, wanting to hear Summer's reply.

She shook her head at her friend's suggestion. "No way. He's way too uptight. He had to fold his clothes neatly before we ever made it to the bed. Who does that?"

"Not a guy who can't keep his hands off you, that's for sure."

Ben curled his hands into tight fists. This conversation and the subject of Summer's ex and how he was in bed was giving Ben fits. On the one hand, jealousy ate at him that she'd been with other men, not that he'd been celibate in the time since they were together last. And on the other hand, he was pissed at himself for caring what she'd been up to with other men when he was so determined to keep things between them professional.

Ivy yawned. "I wish I could stay, but I have to meet with a new client in the morning and I'm exhausted."

"And tipsy," Summer said. "I know I am. You're taking an Uber home, right?"

Ivy nodded. "Yep." She took out her phone and arranged for her ride. "Three minutes away." She slid her shoes back onto her feet and rose.

"I appreciate you coming by. You know how much it means to me to know you care." Summer stood and wobbled a bit, the room obviously spinning around her.

A glance at the table told Ben they'd consumed two bottles between them.

She pulled Ivy into a hug. "Thank you."

"I love you, Summer. You know that."

"Love you, too."

Ivy started for the door, then turned back to face Ben. "Bye, bodyguard!"

"Get home safe," he said, meeting her at the door so he could let her out and lock up behind her.

He turned just as Summer tripped on her own feet, giggled, and righted herself. "Oops."

He rolled his eyes, but he couldn't deny she was cute when drunk. "Come on, princess. Bedtime." He strode around the sofa and grabbed her elbow, pulling her along toward the one room he'd been avoiding since taking this job.

Her bedroom.

The shades were drawn, a small lamp on the nightstand lighting up the room. A white ruffled bedspread with a black heart pillow in the center defined the décor, the furniture also white with black accents, a mix of soft femininity and statement pieces.

"I'm tired."

"So let's get you into bed." He turned his back on her and pulled the comforter down over the mattress so she could climb between the cover and the sheets. When he looked back, she stood in her bra and panties.

She was intoxicated, and it wasn't appropriate, but he couldn't tear his gaze away. From her pink-painted toes, up her toned calves and thighs, to the barely there triangle covering her sweet pussy, his gaze lingered before traveling, up and over her stomach and belly button with a small ring attached, to her full breasts, spilling over the lacy cups of her bra.

"I'm ready," she said, weaving as she walked over to where he stood.

God was testing him, no doubt about it.

"Get in," he said through clenched teeth as he patted the mattress.

"Make me," she said in a flirty, teasing voice.

He raised his eyebrows. Really? She was going to push him?

He scooped her into his arms, and while inhaling her sweet scent that made him fucking harder than he already was, he deposited her onto the bed.

She refused to unlink her arms from around his neck and pulled him down on top of her.

She tucked her cheek against his and sighed. "You smell good," she said, turning and pressing a kiss against his cheek.

She smelled better, and his dick was hard as a rock because of it. He tried to lift himself up but she held on tight.

"It's no wonder no other guys lived up to you," she murmured.

Aww, fuck. She was going to kill him.

He wanted nothing more than to rip those tiny panties off her and sink into her wet heat. Short of that, he'd settle for curling himself around her and breathing her in all night long. She threatened his sanity and his common sense. He had the scars from the last time he'd tangled with her and gotten burned. He'd seen the result when his father had gone back for one more chance and paid the price. All solid reasons for him to get the hell out of her bed.

"Come on, princess. Let me up." He pushed harder and levered himself away from her, breaking her hold on him at last.

No sooner had he turned back than she curled into herself and fell asleep. Ignoring the catch in his chest at the sight of her so vulnerable, he pulled the blanket up and over her body, covering her and tucking her in for the night.

Then he shut off the lamp and headed back to the couch for a cold, lonely night's sleep.

SUMMER AWOKE TO a dull throb inside her head, and it hurt to open her eyes. Her mouth tasted like cotton and she groaned. Too much wine. Her bladder felt full, and she pushed off the covers and realized she was wearing her bra and panties. She never slept in her underwear.

And then she remembered Ben walking her into her room and demanding she get into bed.

Make me, she'd said, taunting him. Teasing him.

So he'd grabbed her and put her into bed, and

she'd pulled him down on top of her. "Oh God." She groaned and put her head in her hands.

Well, it could have been worse. She could have stripped completely. It was the only bright side she could find to what had been a completely embarrassing incident.

She changed into an oversized sleep shirt and headed for the bathroom, where she washed up and brushed her teeth. She pulled her hair into a messy bun and gathered her courage around her before heading into the other room to face Ben.

He stood in the kitchen facing the counter, putting frozen waffles into the toaster oven. A pair of athletic pants rode low on his lean hips. He wasn't wearing a shirt, and even his back was muscular, tapering into his waistband.

He must have sensed her because he turned. "Good morning."

"Morning." She felt a heated blush rise to her cheeks. "Listen, about last night—"

He waved, dismissing her words. "Don't worry about it. Want some waffles?"

"Sure." She glanced at the table, surprised to find orange juice already poured for them both. "Thank you."

"I figured you'd wake up hurting. This was the best I could do. I'm not much of a cook. Not even eggs."

"Waffles will be fine. I eat them all the time," she said, touched by his desire to take care of her in some small way.

When the timer went off, he served them both waffles. Maple syrup was on the table, and she realized she was starving. She cut into the waffles, and they ate in silence until they were both finished.

He pushed his plate aside, propped his elbows on the table, and met her gaze. "You were right the other night. It's time we talked."

She swallowed hard. "Okay."

"I should have taken your calls back then, but I was angry, and you were the best candidate to take that anger out on."

She blew out a long breath. "I don't blame you, really. You lost your job. But things between us were ... intense before they blew up, and when you didn't take my calls or reply to my texts, that hurt."

Although they'd had a short period of time together, it had meant something to her. Given how they didn't have much contact with the outside world during the show, and she'd managed to see him often, her time with Ben had been a whirlwind of intensity.

He wrapped his hand around the glass in front of him. "I know. And I regret how I handled it and wish things had ended differently. But that time in my life taught me not to mix business with pleasure. I need to focus on my job, and that means however difficult it is for us to keep our hands to ourselves now, we have to do it."

His words closed any hope she might have been holding out for them to try again. She didn't like it, because she'd been truthful last night when she'd said that no man since had lived up to him. And not just sexually. But she appreciated that he'd spoken to her about things, and she respected both Ben and his work enough to stick to the boundaries he put in place. Even if it did cause a bit of disappointment.

"Don't worry. I won't throw myself at you again," she said, raising her hand in a solemn promise.

A sad smile lifted his lips. "If things were different…" He shook his head. "But they aren't. I'm going to keep you safe, and when this is over, you'll be going out into the world as a huge star. You won't have time to think about me except as someone you once knew before you were famous."

She shook her head, rose, and gathered their plates, taking them to the sink to clean, unable and unwilling to face him, because he was wrong. She'd think about him as more than someone she'd once known. He was the one who'd gotten away.

ONCE BEN LAID things out for Summer, things
relaxed between them. The tension was no longer
thick, and they were able to coexist more easily. But he
had a difficult time trusting in Summer's willingness to
move on as friends. For over a year, his mom had
never moved on, always keeping his father in her back
pocket to fall back on, and his dad had been there …
until he'd lost everything. Because Nate had been
emotionally invested in his wife.

Summer was right when she said things between
them had been intense the first time, and he had been
on the verge of falling for her and falling hard. Losing
his job in a spectacularly humiliating fashion had
brought Ben face-to-face with reality. Getting involved
with Summer had been stupid. And if he fell back into
a relationship with her again, he could end up no
better than his father, abandoned when something
bigger came along. And Summer's *bigger* was on the
horizon.

He had no doubt she'd win this *competition* and take
off into the stratosphere along with Jade Glow and
those like her. The stylist had delivered so many
clothes she'd had to keep a hanging rack in the corner
of her den because her small closet couldn't hold them
all. Everything had been provided by Jade Glow's
public relations team, which was benefitting from
every public performance Summer and Tawny made

during this time, as Jade's name was plastered all over the publicity materials and mentioned by every show host who promoted the ongoing competition.

Summer was on her way to making it big, and soon she wouldn't have time for Ben or the people she'd known along the way. And he didn't want to be left in the dust. Which meant they were going to have to deal with being platonic while he was guarding her delectable body.

Her schedule was sporadic at best. When she wasn't in a studio doing voice-overs, which he listened to, in awe of her talent, she spent time at the gym doing hard-core cardio and weights, the workouts giving her the stamina for her performances.

Watching her move in her tight spandex shorts and tank top, her breasts bouncing despite the sports bra, should not have been a hardship except on his body, which desired her more with every passing minute, mocking him and his need to keep things between them simple. Unfortunately he also had to deal with the many guys who hit on her while she was doing her routine. He was forced to watch from the sidelines, glaring at the men who flirted with Summer and who she claimed were *just friends*.

The woman was oblivious to the desire in those so-called friends' eyes when they looked at her sexy body and gorgeous face. They were attracted to both the outer packaging and her bubbly, welcoming personality. Eventually, some guy was going to come along at the right time and be *the one*, and the thought made him want to growl in frustration.

When she didn't have necessary engagements scheduled, they remained in her apartment because, for safety reasons, he didn't want her running around the city for no good reason, and he was becoming well acquainted with her sofa while he watched TV.

To her annoyance, he prohibited Starbucks trips unless they were already out of the apartment, and since there was one on the corner of her block, she begged him to go in every time they left the building. Another place where men noticed her constantly.

Her next big event was tomorrow, a nightclub opening, where she and Tawny were performing along with meeting and greeting VIPs. Tonight they were ordering in Chinese food, and he hoped she'd let him pick the movie.

"Laundry time!" Summer walked out of her room, plastic basket in hand. "Dirty clothes need to get clean."

He rose to his feet, immediately alert because she was going to be leaving the safety of the apartment. "Where are the machines?"

"Down the hall. I'd say I don't need an escort, but I'm guessing I'm going to have one anyway?" she asked cheekily.

He inclined his head. "Good call." He patted his holstered weapon and took the basket out of her hands.

"I can carry it. I do it all the time." She extended her hands, requesting the heavy load back.

"Sorry. As long as I'm here, get used to having help."

"Thank you." She grabbed her keys and tossed pods of detergent and fabric softener sheets into the basket. "Let's get this going," she said, striding to the door.

"I'll go first." He needed to make certain no one was waiting for her to exit her apartment.

A quick check and he escorted her down the hall, leaning against the open doorway, keeping an eye out for anyone who might be heading into the laundry room while she sorted her clothes.

Of course, with his luck, she was pulling out her bras and panties, putting them inside a mesh bag, treating him to a look at her variety of undergarments. Black with lace trim, beige with bows on the side, even a red bra, which tormented him with images of what she'd look like with her voluptuous breasts filling the cups, her cleavage spilling out for him to see.

A man walked out of a neighboring apartment, basket in hand, headed to the laundry room. Considering he was coming from inside the building, Ben gave him the benefit of the doubt. As much as he wanted to, he didn't frisk the guy before letting him into the communal laundry room, figuring it would be overkill.

He stepped aside, keeping an eye on the guy, who came up next to Summer and placed his basket on top of a neighboring machine, giving Ben a curious look.

"Summer, where have you been hiding?" he asked, his eyes lighting up at the sight of her.

Great. Another admirer. Everywhere Summer went, she was surrounded by leering assholes who wanted to get into her pants. Ben folded his arms across his chest and glared at the preppy-looking guy in khaki shorts and a polo shirt.

"Greg! It's been too long." She pulled him into what Ben considered a too friendly hug, her breasts pressing against his chest for a second before she stepped back.

Ben's skin felt tight as he watched, annoyed and jealous of their interaction.

"I saw you kick ass on TV," Greg said, mouth curving in a smile.

"Really? Aren't you at work in the morning?"

He laughed. "Yeah, but I watch the entertainment shows at night. You're becoming famous. Pretty soon you'll be moving out of this place and taking a bigger, swankier apartment befitting your status."

She rolled her eyes, blushing at the compliment. "I'm perfectly happy here. So how's work?" she asked.

"Doing well. I got a promotion." He straightened his shoulders, and Ben was surprised he wasn't beating his chest. "So when are you going to put me out of my misery and go out with me?" Greg asked, playfully nudging her with his arm.

Ben ground his teeth waiting for her to answer.

Summer glanced away. "Greg, you know I like you, but my life is way too busy right now to commit to dating." She closed the top of the laundry machine, pressed a few buttons, swiped her credit card, and the hum of the machine began to sound.

"How about after things quiet down?" he asked, not giving up.

"Maybe," Summer said, her cheeks still pink from his earlier compliment.

Ben didn't care if she'd said it to pacify Greg, he didn't like that she'd agreed to possibly see him some undetermined day in the future.

Greg moved in closer. "I'll take that as a yes," he said, just proving Ben's unspoken feelings. That he was a smarmy ass, too slick for a woman like Summer.

"Greg—" She hesitated just long enough, giving him time to chime in.

"How about I just ask you again next time we run into each other?"

Ben had had enough of their chitchat. She'd finished her laundry, and as far as he was concerned, they could go back to her apartment.

He cleared his throat. The sound came out sounding more like an annoyed growl. "Time to go," he said, telling himself he was rescuing Summer from an uncomfortable situation. Whether she wanted to be rescued or not.

"Who is that guy?" Greg asked. "I didn't realize he was with you."

"*That* is my bodyguard," Summer said, glancing Ben's way.

He couldn't read her expression, didn't know if she was grateful he'd given her an excuse to leave or annoyed he was interrupting her time with Greg.

"You need security? Is everything okay?" the other man asked.

"None of your business," he said to the nosy man. He glanced at Summer. "You're finished here, so it's time to go." Ben knew he was being a jealous dick, but he couldn't bring himself to care.

Now Summer did shoot him an annoyed glare before turning to the neighbor. "Everything is fine. It's just precautionary but I do need to get going," she murmured. "It was nice seeing you."

Ben grabbed the basket in one hand and Summer's elbow in another and escorted her out of the room, into the hall, and straight for her apartment, closing and locking the door behind them.

SUMMER LET BEN lead her back to her apartment without argument only because she didn't want to make an embarrassing scene in front of her neighbor.

Once they were inside and the door locked, she turned to him. "What the hell is your problem? That was beyond rude behavior!"

Ben placed the basket down on the floor. "He was a pushy, annoying asshole," he muttered, but his face flushed a deep red, telling her he wasn't all that thrilled with his own actions either.

She raised her eyebrows, recalling the way he'd watched her during her interaction with Greg, the obvious scowl and the rolling of his eyes, things he probably hadn't even been conscious of doing.

Realization dawned at why he'd reacted so strongly. "Ben Hollander, you were jealous. Greg asked me out and it bothered you!"

"He wouldn't take no for an answer and that bugged me."

She folded her arms and stepped into his private space. "I. Don't. Believe. You." She poked him in the chest. "Admit it. You were jealous."

"It's not jealousy. It's that everywhere we go, guys

are looking, leering, hitting on you, and you're damned oblivious!"

"No they aren't! Name one place."

"Starbucks. The guy practically has your order ready the second you walk in the door."

"Kevin?"

"You know his name?"

She rolled her eyes at his absurdity. "Of course I do. I practically live there, which is why he memorized my order and probably everyone else's who is a repeat customer."

"The gym."

"Jason is my trainer!"

"How about the man who scans your ID card when you walk in and asks if you'll be his date for Thursday night Bingo?"

"Mel is old enough to be my grandfather." She choked back a laugh.

"Okay then, the guy who makes your protein shake and has an eye on your boobs the entire time?" he asked, voice rising.

"Mac flirts with everyone!"

"You know all their names!"

She blinked at the serious tone in his voice, unable to believe that he noticed whether guys took an interest in her. That it bothered him was at odds with the man who'd dictated the terms of their relationship as bodyguard and client or just friends.

She tamped down the unwanted spark of hope that flared to life inside her at the prospect of his caring leading to something more between them. Sexually she desired him, but on an emotional level, she wanted a relationship with him, too. They had time together, and why not explore the different facets of a romantic connection between them? He'd claimed to need distance, but she was beginning to wonder if he was merely fooling himself about what he truly wanted.

She ran her tongue over her lips, very aware that he followed the movement with his darkened blue eyes.

"Why do you care who I talk to? Who flirts with me? Who I tease back? You said we needed to keep our distance," she reminded him.

"I do. I need distance. I just fucking … can't." And then his mouth was on hers, hard and demanding.

His hands came to her hips and he picked her up. She wrapped her legs around his waist, and he stepped back, pushing her against the wall, his lips never leaving hers. His tongue thrust past the barrier, gliding over hers, tangling and teasing. And his hands slipped beneath her shirt, gliding up, up until his big hand cupped her breast.

She groaned at the unexpected touch, moaned at

the swipe of his rough fingertips beneath the cup of her bra, over her nipple.

He broke this kiss and his lips came down on her neck, pulling the skin into his mouth, nipping at her flesh. "God, Ben." She ground her hips against his hard cock, need spiking through her.

"I want you. I go to sleep wanting you. I wake up wanting you."

A thrill raced through her. This was what she'd been waiting for. The admission that he desired her as much as she did him. His ultimate capitulation.

"But I can't trust myself to keep you safe if I'm distracted by sleeping with you."

Her sex pulsed at the thought of him thrusting inside her. "Aren't you distracted now? By all this building, unfulfilled desire?"

To her disappointment, he slid her down his body, the hard ridge of his erection gliding against her cotton clothes. She registered the touch and softened with need, her panties growing even damper.

"Do you really think you can't do your job if we're sleeping together?" she asked.

"It's not just that." He stepped back. Ran a shaking hand through his hair.

"Surely you don't think I'm going to tell someone and get you fired again." She studied his serious expression, trying to figure out what was holding him back.

"Of course not. It's deeper than that. It's my past, what I've seen with my—"

Before he could explain further, a familiar ring sounded from where her computer sat open on the table by the couch. The FaceTime ringtone indicated she was getting a call, and the only people who'd contact her this way were her parents, who she hadn't spoken to in almost a week.

Her gaze darted from Ben's tortured expression to the computer.

"Go. Take the call."

"But—"

"Go," he insisted, walking into the kitchen and getting lost staring into the refrigerator before taking out a can of soda.

She shook her head. "This isn't finished," she said, heading to take the face-to-face call with her parents. After which, she intended to pin Ben down on why he was pulling away after admitting he didn't want to let her go.

Chapter Five

SUMMER SAT DOWN in front of the laptop and glanced at the screen. Her mother's face stared back. "Hi, Mom!"

She'd been waiting for this call and the chance to tell her parents what had happened on *The Morning Show*. Although she'd had to hire a professional agent for the business side of her life, she hadn't anticipated the changes her actions would cause with the two people closest to her.

Her heart hurt at the physical and emotional distance between herself and the people she loved. Maybe they'd just forgotten her schedule and that's why they hadn't called until now to see how her national television performance had gone.

"We're home!" Her mother smiled, her teeth white against her tan. She looked happy and healthy, and for that, Summer was glad. "We got back the other day and I've been exhausted. Between jet lag and unpacking, it's been just crazy."

"Oh! That's good. I'm glad you're back safely. And I've been wanting to tell you about my performance on *The Morning Show*," Summer said.

"I want to hear all about it, but first let me tell you about the trip! My favorite stop was the island of Santorini. It's the site of one of the largest volcanic eruptions in recorded history. I've never seen a more beautiful sight, all the white structures built into the mountainside." She sighed and even held up her phone to show Summer a picture.

"It's gorgeous," Summer said. She didn't want to seem disinterested or shallow, but she had news of her own. "Mom—"

"It was wonderful. I have to admit I wasn't sure about overseas travel, but I'm so glad I let your father talk me into it! We even rode donkeys down the side of the mountain."

"That's nice. I can't wait to see pictures … and to see you," Summer said, and before she could speak again, her mother went on to relay more about the history of the places she'd seen on her trip, totally self-absorbed and failing to mention coming to visit and to ask about her life.

"Molly, we have to go! We have early dinner reservations soon." Her father's voice sounded in the background.

"Can I talk to Dad?" Summer asked.

"He just walked out to meet me in the car. We'll call you soon, dear. Bye!" The picture went blank with a double beep for emphasis.

Summer sat stunned, staring at the disconnected screen.

Her parents had obviously not only learned to separate business and family, they'd decided not to care about her career at all. No matter how excited they were about their trip, and she understood it was a trip of a lifetime, how could they not acknowledge or ask about the competition? Her singing? Her well-being? She swallowed over the lump in her throat and lowered the laptop screen, clicking it closed.

She loved her life. She understood she was working toward a goal, but sometimes she was just lonely. She pressed a hand to her eyes and held back tears.

She jumped at the feel of a hand on her back.

"Easy," Ben said in a gruff voice.

"I forgot I wasn't alone." She straightened her shoulders, not wanting him to be a witness to her sadness. She'd just pull herself together and forge on.

"Are you okay?" he asked, sympathy in his voice. He'd obviously heard her mention her appearance and her mother's preoccupation with her trip. Her father's disinterest in talking to her.

She swallowed hard. "I'm fine."

"I don't believe you." His hand moved, gliding from her shoulder to the back of her neck, moving her hair aside so he could massage her tight muscles. "Things have changed between you and your folks since the time you were on *Star Power*. Want to talk about it?"

"What's the point?" she asked.

"You might feel better."

She braced her hands on her thighs and tried not to focus on how sensuously good his fingers felt pressing into her skin, molding her flesh in an attempt to relax and settle her down. In one way, he accomplished his goal. His touch took her out of her own head and made her forget about being upset with her parents, but she doubted he'd intended the physical reactions he inspired. The awareness now searing along her flesh, her nipples tightening, arousal trickling through her veins.

She closed her eyes and imagined those talented hands working their way around to her breasts, cupping her heavy mounds in his hands, and kneading the supple flesh. Plucking and pulling at her already hardened nipples until the desire ran straight to her sex, her clit a hard, pulsing knot of need.

"You're relaxing," he said, those fingers working magic and weaving a sensual spell.

If he only knew.

"Now talk to me. What happened between you and your parents?"

She blinked and her apartment's familiar surroundings came back into focus. Her body still buzzed with arousal, but she forced herself to concentrate on reality, not fantasies Ben wouldn't be making come true.

She sighed and began to explain. "While I was on *Star Power*, a performance opportunity came up for right after the cross-country tour, and my parents didn't handle the negotiations professionally. Because of what they considered my *front-runner* status," she said, making air quotes with her hands, "they thought they could push harder and make demands."

"I guess that didn't go over well?" Ben had removed his hands and she felt the loss. He'd shifted apart from her on the sofa, meeting her gaze.

She shook her head. "No. They demanded so much the people in charge gave the opportunity to someone else who was easier to deal with. Who had a real agent." She blew out a long breath. "You know, the irony, it wasn't that the particular performance meant so much to me but what the situation made me realize. The producers on *Star Power* and the even the musicians who took an interest in the talent on the show encouraged me to hire someone who understood how the business really worked."

"So you did."

"Yes."

"And it didn't go over well with Mom and Dad," he correctly surmised.

"Not at all," she murmured, not wanting to revisit the painful conversation she'd had with her mother and father. "But we're family, and I made it very clear I wanted them in my life and involved in my career as far as giving opinions to me and seeing performances. You have to understand they'd been with me since the beginning when I was five and I sang at a local fair. It was always just the three of us."

Not to mention, she'd given up having a normal childhood in order to perform and sing wherever her parents could book her. Friends? She was the odd duck with other kids, not included in get-togethers because she usually had to say no. Eventually the girls stopped asking. So all she really had was her family.

"Did they distance themselves as soon as you told them?" Ben asked.

She curled one leg beneath her and leaned against the back of the couch. "No, in the beginning they tried to be there, but they couldn't seem to draw the line between support and, well, frankly, meddling. They'd call Anna and try to get involved, so I had to ask them to leave my agent to me."

He winced, clearly understanding that had been the

last straw.

"After that, they pulled back. They bought a place in South Carolina, but they still knew what I had coming up and when, and they showed some interest in my career, but it was strained. Then they decided to take a long trip to Europe, and I think they lost themselves there. They had a wonderful time, but they also had the time difference, and they didn't have to think about me or check in on my schedule. But what it comes down to is they can't figure out how to just be my parents." She shook her head and sighed.

He placed his hand over hers. "It sucks when your family isn't what you want them to be."

Something in his tone told her he wasn't just talking about her parents and situation. She glanced at him, looking to read his expression, but he did the stoic, shuttered thing too well, and she was too emotionally drained to question him now.

She rose to her feet. "I'm going to lie down for an hour before I have to get the laundry and deal with dinner," she murmured.

He opened his mouth like he wanted to say something … and then shut it again, obviously satisfied with letting her be. For now, that was just fine with her. First he'd pulled away, then her parents had closed her out. She might have wanted to push Ben on their relationship, but that was before her video chat with her mother and father.

She was too bruised inside to be rejected yet again.

★　★　★

BEN WATCHED AS Summer walked into her room and closed the door behind her. The sound of soft crying reached him and he muttered a curse, but there was nothing he could do. He'd established his boundaries for a reason, but it was hard not to go to her, wrap her in his embrace, and reassure her she wasn't alone.

Her parents were typical stage parents, living through their daughter and liking the control they'd had over her career. With that taken away, they seemed to have withdrawn their love as well, and he hurt for her. Just like he wished his family could have been a cohesive unit, his mother and father in love and raising him, she wished her parents could give her the support she needed.

But he couldn't bring himself to break down those walls and tell her about his parents' marriage and how his father had basically given up, walking away from a lucrative business and his friends after his mother had betrayed him twice. Or how his dad was a shell of the man he used to be because he hadn't been able to bounce back after the betrayal. Or how much his father's decline had imprinted itself on Ben's psyche and how he handled his life.

She'd ended up sleeping through dinner, so he'd locked her safely in her apartment and thrown her laundry into the dryer, then collected the clothes and brought them back to the apartment. She'd thanked him, and she seemed brighter and happier the next day. He didn't think she was fine. Nobody put pain behind them easily, but she'd moved on, and he was glad she was more like herself again.

It made it easier for him to focus on work, which was his goal tonight. Summer's club opening and the mingling that would follow required his full concentration. Keeping any client safe in a crowded room was always a challenge, and the way Summer distracted him, he needed all his faculties fully engaged.

He waited in the family room, having already changed for the night. Wearing a pair of black dress pants and a black button-down shirt and a jacket that hid his weapon, he was ready to go.

The sound of a door opening had him turning in time to see Summer step out of her bedroom in a white floor-length gown cut low in the front, exposing her delectable cleavage, a slim fit that outlined her curves and had a high slit up one thigh, revealing creamy skin. Her hair fell around her beautifully made-up face in perfect waves. He wanted to kiss her pink pouty lips with a need that bordered on desperation.

"Fuck, princess, you take my breath away." The

words escaped before he could censor them.

A wide smile that could eclipse the sun took hold, and she beamed at him. "Thank you. You dress up pretty nicely yourself, bodyguard," she said with a wink, using the name Ivy had bestowed on him.

"Thank you." He pushed aside the pleasure her words brought him. Work. He needed to focus on work.

She walked up to him, her wildflower scent pervading his senses, and he was grateful for the jacket that covered his body's reaction to her. At a glance, he realized she was wearing high heels because she nearly reached his height, a perfect fit if he were to pull her into his arms.

"Are you ready to go? There's a car waiting downstairs," he said in a roughened voice.

She nodded.

Unable not to be a gentleman, he extended his arm, and she hooked her elbow in his and he led her out into the hallway.

The club, named Echo, vibrated with sound as soon as they stepped past the line of partygoers waiting to get in and the bouncers and then went into the entryway.

Both Summer and Tawny had separate makeup stations in the corners of a dressing room, which was made even more crowded by Tawny's traveling friend group and the addition of security, Ben, and the other woman's bodyguard.

"Summer, you're up!" a female voice called. They'd already been informed Summer would be the first to entertain the audience.

She drew a deep breath and rose from the seat in front of the mirror, looking every bit the elegant princess. "Here goes."

Ben was by her side in an instant. "Break a leg, beautiful."

She treated him to a breathtaking smile before spinning on her heel and heading out to perform.

He closed his eyes and muttered a soft curse for his careless if not true words before following her out of the room and into the flashing strobes of the club. Purple lighting made seeing well from a distance difficult, and he knew he'd have to stick close to Summer in order to maintain her safety. Even if it challenged his very sanity to be by her side and keep his hands to himself.

SUMMER FELT LIKE a goddess. She'd never worn such an expensive dress and shoes, never had a gown fitted to her frame so there were no gaps or dips in the fabric. She'd glided on air walking into Echo on Ben's arm, having to keep reminding herself that he was there as her bodyguard and not as her date.

He looked hot in all black, his facial hair a sexy scruff that needed shaving, but she was glad he'd opted to leave it alone.

She only had to perform two songs, one ballad and another with a fast tempo and beat. She did her thing, singing and dancing, knowing Jade Glow's people were in the audience watching her, judging her, and after Tawny's set, they would be comparing them. Yet despite the importance of her performance and all that was riding on her doing well, all she could focus on was the man in the audience there to do a job.

From the moment she stepped onto the stage to perform, she was aware of Ben's muscular arms folded across his chest, his heavy-lidded gaze shifting between her and the crowd, alert and aware the entire time. She sang more to him than the audience, at least in her mind, and she couldn't deny the fact that when his gaze was on her, he ate her alive, his desire for her a potent and almost tangible thing despite his protestations that he couldn't let himself get involved. He never had explained his reasons, and the time had never been right to bring up the conversation again.

She finished on a high and accepted the applause before striding off the stage and handing the microphone to the woman in charge. Tawny went immediately after her, as usual nailing everything about her moment in the spotlight. After her performance, she met up with her entourage, including her agent, as usual.

Instead of standing around, Summer swung past them, head held high, and headed for the dance floor.

"Where are you going?" Ben tugged her back against his hard body.

"I want to dance." The deejay had begun to spin more music, and the beat was thrumming inside her.

"Well, I'm not letting you out of my sight," he said with an irritable glance at the crowded dance floor.

She raised one shoulder and shrugged. "Guess that means you're going to have to dance with me." She slid her hand into his and pulled him into the crowd.

Thanks to the amount of people, they would have been pushed together for even a fast dance, but the music shifted, and any movement would now be slow. She intended to take advantage, but before she could act, someone bumped her from behind, shoving her into the person across from her, which nearly caused a domino effect of people knocking into each other.

Ben grabbed her, pulled her against him, and began to sway to the music. She tipped her head back, and their gazes locked as they moved in perfect unison. It was too loud for them to talk unless they wanted to shout to be heard, so their sensual movements spoke for them. She had one hand on his shoulder, his arm wrapped around her back, her chest pressed against his, and the hardness of his lower body caused an arousing sense of awareness in hers. He smelled delicious, the masculine scent she associated with him adding to the variety of sensations overtaking her.

Without taking his gaze off hers, he lowered his head ever closer to hers, his lips brushing her mouth one, twice, three times before he licked at the seam with his tongue. She moaned, not that he would hear, and parted her lips, letting him inside.

He tightened his hold, pressing their bodies intimately, hips grinding together to the beat of the music, his pelvis rocking against hers, the sparks of arousal spiking inside her.

She was happy to let the music provide the beat while she and Ben danced sensuously against each other, a subtle shifting and grinding that was hidden by the many people surrounding them.

He lifted his head, meeting her gaze, desire and raw need in his expression, when suddenly Tawny's loud voice sounded near their ears. "Well, well, well, just like old times."

Ben immediately stepped back, putting space between them though not letting go of his hold on Summer; however, she knew at this moment, thanks to Tawny's interruption, it was her safety keeping them close, not his desire to be near her. If the way Ben dragged her off the dance floor was any indication, he didn't appreciate the reminder of their problematic past.

Tawny was obviously determined to do more than take away Summer's chance at a career-changing opportunity. She wanted to cause as much trouble as she possibly could. Anything to throw Summer off her game. The joke was on Tawny, because Summer could handle the other woman and her bitchy games.

She just needed to figure out how to get through to Ben, because nobody got lost in a moment like they'd had if he wasn't yearning to be together again. He was fighting himself, and she needed him to stop.

For now, though, she figured Ben needed time to stew and be angry at himself for kissing her instead of guarding her, so Summer strode ahead of him into the dressing room area. She'd left her purse with her lipstick and gloss in a drawer of the vanity. She wanted to touch up her makeup since her lips felt damp after her gloss had been licked off by Ben.

She approached the area to which she'd been assigned, finding it empty, no people hanging around, but when she reached her mirrored section, she stopped short. All her things were strewn everywhere. A vase of flowers, which had been on the counter, was lying randomly across the floor, surrounded by shards of broken glass. The drawers were open, and her purse had been removed and emptied out, the contents mixed among the flowers.

And someone had written on the mirror with what looked like lipstick, the words DROP OUT OR ELSE scrawled in red on the reflective surface. This was the first time she'd had visible proof that there was a threat of some kind against her, and she was freaked out.

Summer spun around in a panic and ran directly into Ben's hard chest.

"Whoa," he said, grasping her forearms tightly. He glanced beyond her, taking in the wreckage of what had been her backstage area.

"Fuck. Who the hell was watching this room?" he yelled, keeping Summer tucked protectively beneath the shelter of his arm.

And she didn't want to leave there anytime soon.

BEN WAS FURIOUS. His job was to guard Summer, not to danger-proof the club. Either someone hadn't done *their* job or the powers that be thought it was enough to have coverage on the girls, to hell with other types of threats. He wouldn't be surprised if it was the latter. Orion Motors and Jade Glow just wanted the talent protected.

Speaking of the talent, Summer had curled into him for protection, and he hated to admit how much he liked her there, about as much he'd liked that hot kiss and grind on the dance floor. He ran a hand through his hair. Something had to be done about this attraction between them, or at least his on-again, off-again reaction, but now wasn't the time for him to dwell on what.

The club manager, who had introduced himself earlier, walked over to Ben. He took in the situation at a glance and groaned. "Shit."

Ben frowned at the man. "Did you have anyone keeping an eye on this room and the women's belongings?"

He shook his head. "I'm so sorry, sir, but we didn't. People could have come and gone all night."

This was why a bodyguard was often only half of the equation. Obviously nobody was paying for investigative services. They'd just reported the initial threat to the police and hired Ben.

"Call the cops. Now."

He glanced at Summer, who had pulled herself together and was watching the interaction between them. "Do you think they'll find anything helpful?" she asked as the manager stepped aside to make the call.

"No." His gut told him they wouldn't discover prints that would lead to a culprit. Just everyone and anyone who'd had access to this room, which was the entire club. A couple could have snuck in here for a quickie and the girl fixed herself up after. Anything could have happened in here in between the time of the act and when they'd walked in.

"The police will be here soon," the manager said.

Ben glanced up at the ceiling, looking for signs of video cameras and finding none. "I don't suppose you have cameras covering the room?" he asked the other man.

"No." He shoved his hands into his pants pockets. "Look, I need to greet the cops when they show up."

Ben inclined his head. "Go. But you need to re-think your security," he muttered, disgusted with the situation.

For the next few hours, the police came in and handled things, talking to the employees who had access to the room, questioning Tawny and members of her entourage, but overall, informing Ben and Summer they'd come up empty. There were too many people in the club to bother fingerprinting the area, and Tawny and her friends denied having done anything wrong. The cops documented the incident, but there was nothing more they could do.

Summer looked ready to collapse from exhaustion, and Ben turned to the cop in charge. "I'm taking Ms. Michelle home. If you need us, you have her information."

"Go ahead," the officer said.

Ben pulled out his cell and called the driver, asking him to meet them at the front of the club.

Then he turned to Summer and met her gaze, the first time they'd been alone since the moments on the dance floor. Soft black smudges looked like light bruises beneath her eyes, makeup and exhaustion combining to cause the vulnerable look.

He brushed a gentle knuckle across her cheek. "Hey. Are you okay? Because I'm not going to let anyone near you. You know that, right? You're safe."

She nodded, gazing up at him with wide brown eyes. "I'm really fine. I just don't understand why anyone would be desperate for me not to win. Other than Tawny, who cares?" She bit down on her lower lip. "Do you think she's capable of this? Because I don't want to think that someone I know could do something like that. I mean, I know she's ambitious, but this is crazy." She gestured to the mess behind her.

Ben groaned. "I honestly wouldn't rule her out. She's caused trouble for you before. You believe she's the one who turned you in to the producers hoping they'd let you go and she'd have one less person to compete with in *Star Power*." Ben raised an eyebrow. "Which means she's incredibly competitive and determined to win. At all costs."

Summer sighed. "At least I have you. And I trust you to take care of me."

Her words were humbling and they meant something to him. He wouldn't take them, or the job he was hired to do, lightly.

Chapter Six

BEN COULDN'T SLEEP. Not with thoughts of Summer circling in his brain. You'd think it would be her safety that concerned him, but he trusted in his abilities to protect her from any outside danger. Instead it was their relationship that had him tossing and turning. He couldn't keep his hands to himself when she was around. If it were just the physical attraction that was palpable between them, he could tuck it into his back pocket and ignore it while doing his job, but over the days he'd been with her, he'd come to realize the fact that Summer was his ideal woman.

Her independence was a turn-on. Daily, she proved that, although she missed having her family around her, she could handle herself in the city and on the job. He admired her drive to succeed and go after what she wanted in life with determination and gusto.

Her talent was exceptional. When she sang, he got

lost in the emotion behind the music, and her voice transported him out of his head and to a place where he could focus only on her. It would be a huge loss if she couldn't see her dream of performing for a living come to fruition.

Then there was the feminine vulnerability she exuded. The soft and sweet woman inside, a woman who, despite her independence, valued her family, and though she'd never admit it, a part of her was a lonely girl who wished for the time to make friends. He'd seen the way she looked at Tawny and her girl pack. She didn't like those women, but she envied their closeness, though not the meanness that brought them together.

It was that sweet woman he couldn't jerk around anymore, giving her mixed signals about what he wanted from her. Because he knew damn well what he desired. The question was whether or not he could have it ... and still let her go when the job came to an end and she took off for a bigger, brighter life.

AFTER EVERYTHING THAT had happened at Echo Nightclub, Summer couldn't sleep. She still couldn't quite process that the threat against her was real. Sure, she'd had Ben living here, and that should have been enough for her to take things seriously, but not until she'd seen the warning in lipstick had she been *scared*.

But Ben said he wouldn't let anyone near her, and she believed him. His words and fierce protectiveness made her breathe more easily. Besides, she wasn't about to let anyone stand in the way of her dreams finally coming true. She couldn't imagine what she would do if this opportunity slipped through her fingers and went to Tawny. For the first time, she'd have to take a good look at her life and decide what kind of realistic career she wanted to have. Voice-overs were lucrative for now, but could she count on them long term? Did she need to consider returning to college?

She shuddered and refused to dwell on it, because having to do so meant she'd failed. And she didn't think that way. Ever. She never had. From the time she was a little girl, all she'd wanted to do was perform. And she would succeed doing it, no matter what whoever wanted her gone from the competition thought. She wasn't dropping out.

And she had Ben to look out for her, which brought her to the next reason she couldn't sleep. Their sensual dance had heightened her awareness of the man, and she had no doubt in the moment he'd felt the same way. It was only when he had time to think that he pulled away.

Which meant she couldn't give him that time.

She rubbed her hands together and paced her room, debating doing what her body was begging her to do—walking into the other room and seducing Ben. On his own, he'd never come to her, and they weren't alone except in her apartment. If she didn't take advantage now, she was wasting precious time to be with him. Time that would be ticking down if she did win the competition and went off on a world tour. Time she could have been spending with him.

She didn't own a negligee, but she had something much better and more enticing, she hoped. She had her body.

She looked down at her oversized tee shirt, gathered her courage, and walked out of her room.

BEN ROLLED OVER, jarred from sleep by a warm presence in his bed. A soft hand slid over his chest and down his stomach, inching lower, toward his now erect dick.

"What are you doing?" he asked Summer in a gruff voice filled with sexual need.

"Going after what I want," she murmured. "And I want you."

He groaned, wondering how he was supposed to resist her. She smelled like flower-scented body wash, a fragrant reminder of their shared erotic past. Times when he'd slid deep inside her slick channel and lost himself to her in their short but intense affair. One that had ended badly.

As that wayward hand stroked ever closer to his aching cock, he tried to remind himself that he didn't want to repeat past mistakes like his father had, and that this woman made him do stupid things. Like get involved with a contestant and violate his security contract.

And now she was the client of a firm he really liked working for. Although there were no contractual rules to violate, there was the moral notion of not having sex with a woman he was protecting.

"This is not a good idea," he said to remind her as much as himself that they were dangerous together.

"Says you. I say stop thinking so hard." As she spoke, she slipped her hand into his boxer briefs and wrapped her fingers around his aching shaft.

He let out a low groan, the pleasure incredible and actively short-circuiting his brain cells. All the reasons to keep his distance fled in the wake of her tempting touch. If she kept this up, he'd come in her hand, and that wasn't something he was willing to let happen.

Acknowledging she'd won this round, he pushed himself up and flipped her onto her back, coming over her, his hands braced on either side of her shoulders. Her dark hair fanned out against the white pillow, and he met her gaze, taking in her dilated pupils and the stark need in her expression.

No man could resist her pull. "Fuck it," he said and lowered his mouth to hers, slicking his tongue over her lips, taking in everything that was Summer.

She kissed him back, arching up and into him as her soft tongue met his. Control lost, he ground his hips against hers, his cock hard and demanding relief. The bed, a pullout without the ability to support their weight and motions, began to creak, sounding like the mattress would go crashing down with the next thrust of his lower body.

He groaned and broke the kiss. "We need to move this into your bed before we end up on the floor."

She licked at the moisture on her lips and nodded. "Works for me."

He pushed himself up and off the flimsy mattress and held out his hand, pulling her up and getting his first glimpse of her naked body. Summer was toned from her workouts at the gym, but she had soft, cushiony curves he adored, with full breasts and generous hips she had no problem embracing. The urge to run his hands over those curves was strong, but the desire to be skin to skin with her again was greater.

He led her toward the bedroom, and while she crawled onto the bed, he stripped off his boxer briefs, his erection springing free at last. A glance at the bed and he saw Summer, her pale, beautiful body waiting for him, her dusky nipples pulled into tight peaks, her pussy trimmed and slick with desire.

He'd been waiting for this moment, not wanting to admit to himself just how badly he desired her. But he was here and he wasn't capable of pulling back.

He climbed onto the mattress beside her. "I want to lick every delectable inch of you."

"Then what are you waiting for?" she asked, her voice husky and desire-laden.

Planning to start at the top and work his way down, he cupped her breast in his hand and drew one nipple into his mouth, pulling on the tight peak. She tasted sweet, like candy, and he laved, suckled, and tongued until she was writhing with need, her hips bucking upward with every drag of his tongue. He spent a long while on one nipple before moving on and sliding his mouth to the other breast. He held the heavy mound in his hand as he treated it to the same sensual assault.

Only when she was desperate for more did he lick his way down the center of her chest, past her rib cage, and down to her belly button, tangling his tongue in the piercing there before heading lower still.

Grasping her thighs, he pulled her legs apart and settled between them. He glanced up, their gazes met, and a rush of heat swept through him at the look of anticipation in her expression and the yearning in her eyes. His cock throbbed against the mattress, but he was determined to watch her come at least once before he lost himself inside her.

He slid his fingers over her damp folds and parted her sex, the little bud of her clit peeking out at him. With a rough groan, he dipped his head and slicked his tongue over her sex.

She shuddered at the first swipe. And when he settled in and teased her with his lips and tongue, alternating feather-light touches and harder nibbles with gentle grazes of his teeth, she began to chant his name and try to grab on to the bedding with her hands, unable to find anything to hold on to and ground her.

He kept up his assault, taking her to the brink once, twice, then a third time, letting the waves of desire subside without allowing her to find release.

She grabbed his hair and moaned. "Ben, please, please, please. I need to come."

And he was ready to let her.

He teased her clit with his tongue, this time with deliberate pressure, as he slid a finger inside her at last, curling it upward and finding that spongy place he hoped would bring her over the edge—and it worked.

She pulled at his hair and cried out, bucking her

hips as he held her in place with his free hand, guiding her through her orgasm with the hard press of his tongue. As she came down, he lifted his head and glanced at her face. Cheeks flushed, eyelids closed, her body trembling.

It was a glorious sight. She quaked with the aftershocks of her orgasm as he raised himself over her, his cock gliding over her still-sensitive sex.

He guided himself to her entrance and stilled, cursing inside his head. "Condoms. I think I have some in my travel bag."

"Then what are you waiting for?" she asked, eyes glittering with renewed need.

He pushed off her and headed for the other room before returning with two condoms in hand. He quickly sheathed himself, rejoining her on the bed and sliding between her legs.

He cupped his hand around his shaft and notched the head of his cock at the entrance of her slick pussy. "Damn, but I want you badly."

She bent her knees in response. "So take me. I'm yours."

He didn't need an engraved invitation. Hands braced, he raised his hips and plunged deep, the feel of her slick channel clasping him tight in heat nearly sending him over right then. He gritted his teeth and held back, giving her time to adjust before he began to move, picking up a steady rhythm with ease.

He made the mistake of meeting her gaze while thrusting into her, and emotions he wanted locked down rose inside him. They'd always had an intense connection, and that hadn't changed, but he had no intention of falling for her that way again. He knew from experience it was a short distance to fall. The easiest solution?

He pulled out and spoke in a rough tone. "Hands and knees, princess."

Her gaze darkened, and she complied immediately, treating him to the gorgeous sight of her sleek back, dark hair in stark contrast to her fair skin, and firm but rounded ass. His dick throbbed painfully, and he used his knee to spread her legs wider apart, positioning himself behind her before taking her hard.

She moaned as he possessed her, the feelings swamping him as strong as before, but at least he didn't have to meet her gaze and have her see and know how much she affected him.

Gathering her hair in his hand, he anchored himself as he pumped his hips in and out, his hard dick gliding through her as he moved. He wasn't going to hold out for long, and from the sounds coming from deep in her throat, neither was she. As he felt his balls draw up and his climax near, he slid a hand around her hip and glided his fingertips over her damp clit.

She gasped and began a slow chanting of his name,

her back arching and her body accepting of every slam of his hips, until his name became a prayer, and the prayer a scream as she came, her orgasm triggering his own. He came hard, spilling everything inside him. Wrung dry, he collapsed on top of her, her warmth seeping into his skin.

He was spent and done for. Not wanting to crush her, he rolled off her. Her cheek was pressed into the mattress, her eyes closed, her breath coming in shallow gasps from her slightly parted lips. Acting on impulse, he leaned over and pressed his lips to hers.

He felt her mouth curl into a smile. "That was so good," she whispered in an exhausted voice.

He couldn't stop the grin that hit his lips. "It was fucking fantastic."

"When can we do it again?" she asked.

He laughed. "When you can take a normal breath."

She giggled, her eyes remaining closed, that sated, satisfied smile still in place.

As he studied her, he realized how deluded he'd been.

He'd changed positions, thinking not seeing her face would keep him more grounded. Except he'd been wrong. Sleeping with her again had pulled him in deeper, feelings he didn't want to experience again fighting to spring free.

Which meant one thing. He was well and truly fucked. In more ways than one.

Chapter Seven

SUMMER KEPT UP a healthy exercise routine, which was why it shocked her that Ben had worn her out. She woke up the next morning to the sun streaming through the window in her bedroom. She patted the sheet beside her and found it cool, Ben obviously long gone.

She wasn't surprised. She figured he didn't appreciate being ambushed by a naked woman in his bed, and he'd withdrawn in order to regroup. Too bad for him, she had no intention of giving him space, and in her tiny apartment, he couldn't go far anyway. Not without her, as it was his job to guard her, night and day.

Not in the least bit discouraged, she headed for the bathroom and brushed her teeth. She showered and took a nice, long hot one, cleaning up with her favorite flower-scented body wash and shampoo. She pulled on an easy floral dress, braided her hair, decided to forego makeup, and went to find Ben.

He stood at the window, wearing his black athletic pants and no shirt, sunlight, blue clouds, and the cityscape in the background. She drooled at the sight of his muscled back and arms, and had an immediate memory of him taking her last night, his strong body covering her back, his thick cock bringing her ultimate pleasure.

She swallowed hard, arousal coming to life inside her again.

She realized he'd dialed his phone and put it to his ear.

She stepped back to give him some privacy when he spoke.

"Hey, Ava."

Ava? A spark of jealousy surged through Summer at the mention of another woman's name and the fondness in his tone.

"I have bad news," he said. "I'm going to have to cancel this weekend."

Summer took his words like a punch in the stomach. He had plans with this woman? Was she the reason he wanted to keep his distance and kept pulling away? She'd pushed him into sleeping with her last night, and a wave of nausea took hold.

Summer swallowed hard, knowing she ought to turn around and leave, not listen in on a private conversation. Eavesdropping was wrong but her feet remained planted firmly on the floor.

"I know," he went on. "I was looking forward to it, too, but duty calls."

And that's what she was to him, Summer thought, her stomach rolling. A job. Nothing more. Tears prickled in her eyes as she realized she'd let herself begin to care. She shouldn't have pushed him, and she didn't need to hear any more.

She spun around, intending to run back to her room, but she slipped on the hardwood floor. She grabbed for the nearest thing to stop her fall, muttering a shriek as her palm hit the corner of the wall and pain shot through her hand before she fell down in a humiliating heap.

"Shit. Ava, gotta call you back." He strode over to her. "Summer?" Ben loomed over her, staring at her with concern. "You okay?" He held out a hand to help her up.

"I tripped. I mean slipped." Her face flamed with heat as she let him pull her to her feet. "I fell," she said lamely.

"Are you hurt?"

She shook her head. "Nothing but my pride. Go ahead and call your—call Ava back."

A hint of something flashed across his face, but as usual, he was too skilled at hiding his feelings.

He narrowed his gaze. "Please finish that state-ment. You said, 'Go ahead and call your—' My what, Summer? Who do you think Ava is to me?" he asked, his voice taking on what sounded like a … hurt edge.

"How should I know?" she hedged, knowing she didn't have long before she'd have to confess.

"You don't have to *know*," he said. "You just need to tell me what went through your mind."

She pouted, pursing her lips together hard before forcing out the words. "Well, you don't have a sister, so I assume Ava is your girlfriend."

He cocked an eyebrow, a true angry scowl on his handsome face. "You think so little of me that you believe I'd sleep with you if I had a girlfriend?" He folded his arms across his chest in a defensive gesture. "I'm offended, Summer."

She winced, realizing he was right. She'd taken his absence this morning as deliberate, heard his call to a woman, and jumped to all the worst possible conclu-sions.

"I'm sorry." She wrapped her arms around her waist. "That wasn't nice of me. It's just that I heard you say her name and I was—"

"Jealous?" he asked, nailing the unwanted, embar-rassing emotion.

"Yes," she admitted.

His gaze softened. "Thank you for being honest."

He reached out and tapped her nose. "But the fact is, you have no reason to be. You consume my thoughts, and my body craves only you."

Her mouth went dry, and her panties immediately grew damp at his light touch and seductive words. "Oh."

"My days of pulling away are over. Next time I kiss you or put my hands on you, I won't be stopping."

"But … you weren't in bed when I woke up, so I assumed you had second thoughts, considering I snuck into your bed last night."

"My boss called and I didn't want to wake you, so I answered out here. Then I made us coffee." He gestured toward the kitchen. "Summer, listen." He grasped both her hands in his. "I'm a grown man. I own my choices. You might have crawled into my bed, but I wanted you, too. And I can admit, I can't resist you now."

BEN HAD HAD time to think while Summer slept, and he knew he had to come to terms with his need and desire for her. He might not want to repeat past mistakes, might not want to be like his old man, might not want to deal with the inevitable heartbreak when she left on a world tour and became a superstar … but he couldn't resist her. And that little fact, although it didn't change his fears, superseded them. As long as they came to an understanding about what this thing between them was … and wasn't.

At his admission, her eyes opened wide and her mouth parted in a sexy little O. He couldn't help but chuckle at her astonished expression, not that he blamed her. She had every right to think he had been withdrawing from her. And though a part of him wanted to do just that and protect his heart, he couldn't keep doing the push-pull dance that hurt her. Hell, it hurt them both.

As much as he owed her an explanation for his earlier behavior, it entailed a gut-wrenching, reaching-into-his-soul accounting of why he'd kept his distance to begin with. And Ben didn't like to revisit his childhood and his parents' marriage, mostly because watching things play out between them hurt and had ultimately skewed his views on life and love.

He reached up and pulled her down from her perch on the sofa, toppling her onto the cushions alongside him. Her fragrant scent wafted over him as she righted herself and adjusted into a sitting position and smoothed a hand over her damp braided hair.

"You're in a very good mood this morning."

He laughed. "Because I had fantastic sex last night and I'm anticipating even better this morning. I just want to get something straight between us."

"What would that be?" she asked.

"This is sex. Great sex. Hot sex. But just sex all the same. You're going to be embarking on a huge career, and I'm not looking for anything serious. Are we in agreement?" he asked.

She treated him to a jerky nod and he hated the vulnerable look that flashed over her face. "Great sex. I can handle that."

Before he could reply, his cell phone rang.

He shot her a regret-filled look and pulled the phone from his back pocket, answering the call. "Hollander."

His boss was on the other end. "What's up?" Ben asked.

"Heard you canceled the party at my place," Dan said, not sounding happy.

He always hosted a get-together for his employees' birthdays and holidays, his home the gathering place for anyone who didn't have a family or those who wanted to celebrate with friends instead. Dan had his reasons for declaring holidays celebration worthy, and Ben understood them even if he wasn't the celebrating type.

"It's just a birthday. They come around every year. We can postpone it or skip it altogether," Ben said in what he knew would be a futile attempt at bailing on his own party.

Dan's next words ensured that Ben would be there no matter what.

"Yes, sir," Ben said with the utmost amount of respect. "We'll be there." With a groan, he disconnected the call.

"What's wrong?" Summer asked, curling her legs beneath her.

"Question for you," he said, not answering hers. This weekend they had a trip to Atlantic City for a hotel performance, but nothing till then. "I didn't see anything on your schedule for tomorrow. Are you still free?"

She nodded. "Why?"

He propped an elbow on the top of the sofa, his arm close to hers. "What you heard on the phone earlier was me telling Ava to cancel a birthday party the people I work with were planning."

"For you?" she asked, surprised.

"For me. Tomorrow is my birthday," he said with reluctance.

"Ben! Why didn't you say something?" she asked, a little bit of hurt in her voice. "I'd have bought or made a cake! Birthdays are important."

Which was why he hadn't told her. "Birthdays were never a big deal to me. Well, maybe they were when I was younger, but when my parents' marriage went south, all the family celebrations ended." He eyed her carefully, wondering if she'd judge him for how screwed up his family was.

She came from what he considered a functional family unit, two parents, happily married, with a daughter they doted on. Well, until she'd disappointed them by cutting them out of her career decisions. Come to think of it, maybe they weren't all that functional after all. Maybe nobody came from the perfection he wished he could have had. Still, Ben's dad had set an example of how a man should be careful with the choices he made. Putting Summer in a no-serious-relationship zone made perfect sense.

Summer placed a comforting hand on his arm, her soft fingers searing his skin, forcing those thoughts out of his mind. "What happened?" she asked.

He swallowed hard. "It's not important."

Her pretty pout did nothing to dissuade him from not discussing his past.

"Fine. You're off the hook. For now."

He nodded, his relief huge. "Back to tomorrow, the people I work with are big on parties for all occasions. So that was my boss, Dan Wilson, who got the message from Ava that I wanted to cancel, and he isn't letting that happen."

"I agree with him. You should celebrate your birthday with your friends. I'll be fine here. I promise not to leave the apartment while you're gone."

She sounded sincere, and he appreciated that she wanted him to be with his friends. But that wasn't the plan. "That's not what Dan suggested."

Or what Ben wanted, which was why he'd pulled the plug on the thing to begin with.

"You are not staying here alone. Dan takes protection very seriously, as do I. But he lost his wife to cancer awhile back, and because of that, he believes in living life to the fullest."

"That's so sad," she murmured. "But so sweet at the same time."

Dan would have a heart attack at being called sweet, although that's what he was, deep down inside.

"It is. And Dan said, and I quote, 'Life's short. We're having your party. Just bring the girl.'"

Summer gaped at the suggestion.

Ben understood. He'd canceled because he was working, and bringing Summer around his colleagues and friends was too intimate even for people already sleeping together. Sure, he'd decided to allow himself this time with Summer, but he also needed to keep his heart protected. Bringing her into his inner circle of friends and life wouldn't help him in that regard.

"Go with you? No." She waved a hand in dismissal. "You go on and I'll be safe and sound right here." She patted the sofa for emphasis.

He shook his head and groaned. "Sorry but I can't

do that. Dan's the boss. He said to bring you. You said you have no plans. Which means we're going to a barbeque tomorrow at noon."

Even if she wasn't any keener on getting up close and personal with Ben's life than he was with letting her. They didn't have a choice.

SUMMER TAPPED HER foot nervously against the floorboard of the Uber they were taking to Ben's boss's house. He sat beside her in silence. She'd chosen a floral casual dress for the occasion, and unlike her trips to the gym or the studio for work, she had no intention of documenting her day for social media. Ben's friends and his day were off-limits to the prying public.

She was nervous about going to the birthday party for Ben because she didn't know his friends and wasn't sure she belonged there. Until yesterday, she'd had no idea when Ben's birthday even was. After he'd been fired from *Star Power*, she'd attempted to do the obligatory postmortem stalking of her ex only to discover he didn't have a social media presence. No photos to torture herself with and no birthdate mentioned online for her to see.

She did, however, have a photo of them stuck in her wallet, a selfie she'd coerced him into taking while they were sharing ice cream, and which she'd had printed so she could look and mourn what might have been. He didn't need to know that though.

She'd been wrong in thinking he wanted to regroup and pull away the morning after. Instead he seemed to have come to terms with the fact that the desire between them was off the charts and ignoring it wasn't going to work. He had, however, put an emotional wall up between them, and she really couldn't blame him. They might be in a good place when it came to *them*, sex being a good icebreaker, but they weren't a couple in the true sense of the word.

She glanced out the window at the typical New York traffic on the highway and sighed.

Ben closed his hand over hers. "Relax. It's just the people I work with. They're nice and you'll feel comfortable."

"Thank you," she murmured, turning toward him. "And I promise I won't do anything to let them know we … hooked up or whatever. I don't want to get you into trouble again." She glanced away, knowing that despite apologies given, that was still a sore subject for him.

A wry smile pulled at his mouth, which on Ben became the equivalent of a sexy grin. "If I know Dan, he wouldn't be surprised. Trust me when I tell you, there's nothing traditional about this group. They mix family and business, but I don't think we need to give them things to gossip about, either."

She nodded in understanding. "Agreed." She'd handle this however he wanted to and take her cues from him.

"What else is on your mind?" he asked.

She didn't want to admit to her nerves. She handled large audiences. She'd deal with his friends. "I couldn't get you a gift," she said instead.

And she really did feel bad. She'd found out about the event less than twenty-four hours before it was to take place, and she was house-bound as dictated by her bodyguard, the birthday boy himself.

He leaned an arm on the back seat. "I don't need presents. I don't even want a party."

"Well, it sounds like you were outvoted, so you might as well enjoy it."

"I intend to. I hope you will, too. At least you're getting out of your apartment and going to a place where you don't have to worry about anyone getting near you. It's a house full of bodyguards."

She laughed. "Good point."

The car pulled up to a modest house with white siding, a well-manicured green lawn, and SUVs parked along the street and in the driveway.

Her stomach tumbled as they came to a stop, and not long after, Ben led her to the front door, his strong hand hard and reassuring on her lower back.

He didn't bother ringing the bell, just pushed open the door and urged her to step in alongside him.

She glanced around, taking in the family photos lining the wall in the entryway, giving the place a homey feel. The sound of voices and laughter coming from inside the house drew her in.

"Come this way." Ben tipped his head toward the center of the house, and Summer followed him to an obviously renovated, open-concept kitchen and family room crowded with people. Mostly large men, like Ben, strong and muscular guys, and one woman, who had to be Ava, laughing among them.

"Hey, the birthday boy is here!" A broad-shouldered man with a buzz cut and a collared short-sleeved shirt headed their way. "Happy birthday!" He hooked an elbow around Ben's neck and pulled him in for a fatherly-type hug.

"Thanks. Dan, this is Summer Michelle. Summer, my boss, Dan Wilson."

Dan met her gaze with an assessing one of his own as he extended his hand. "A pleasure to meet you. I trust my boy is doing his job and keeping out of your way at the same time?"

Summer bit the inside of her cheek. "He's only under foot when he needs to be," she said, being discreet as she'd promised. "And it's good to meet you, too." She shook his hand.

"This is my son, Jared," Dan said of the dark-haired man who joined them.

"Hi, Jared." Summer smiled.

"Man, Ben gets all the good assignments," Jared said, not so discreetly looking her over.

Ben cleared his throat. "Watch the eyes, Wilson."

Jared blinked in surprise. "Well, damn. Okay then."

Ava chimed in. "Jared, go away and leave Ben's woman alone," she said, sounding pissed off.

"But… We're not… I mean I'm not Ben's anything." She'd promised she'd keep whatever was between them private, and they'd agreed they weren't anything serious.

Ava grinned, shaking her head at Summer. "Besides, he gave himself away. He bit Jared's head off for just looking, and his hand hasn't left your lower back since you walked into the room. Possessive much?" she asked, smirking at Ben.

A glance told Summer that Ben's cheeks were a bright red from Ava's summary of what was going on between them.

"Happy birthday!" she said, cutting off any reply. She leaned up on her tiptoes and kissed his cheek. "And nice to meet you, Summer. I'm Ava Talbott," the pretty, bubbly woman said.

"Hi. Nice to meet you, too."

The introductions continued with a man named Tate Shaw, who Summer later discovered was originally from Texas and occasionally did work there for McKay Taggart Security, and Austin Rhodes, another of the big bodyguards.

Summer found herself pulled into their warmth, amused by the familial bickering, and over the course of the afternoon, she managed to relax and enjoy herself.

Although the guys gravitated toward each other and hung out together, Ben tried to make sure Summer was comfortable and didn't leave her side—until Ava shooed him away.

"Let us girls talk. Go hang out with the boys."

She met Summer's gaze and rolled her eyes. "Too much testosterone most of the time, and I'm surrounded by it."

"Really? I think you'd enjoy it."

She shook her head and laughed. "Why? Because they're all muscular and hot? They're all like my brothers." She glanced at where the guys congregated.

"It's a tough job to have," Summer said.

"You try dealing with these hardheaded men on a daily basis."

Summer smiled. "That's probably frustrating."

"Let's go sit on the back porch. It's gorgeous out."

Ava led her outside to a deck that overlooked a wooded area with trees.

"It's beautiful here," Summer murmured, the air still warm. They settled into a long porch swing.

"It is." She paused, then said, "I grew up here … well, from my mid-teens on."

"Really? Was your mother married to Dan?" Summer asked, drawing the only conclusion she could.

Ava held back a snort. "Actually Dan lived in a different neighborhood when Jared and I were younger, and back then we were neighbors." She paused and Summer gave her time to gather her thoughts. "My mother was … is an addict. Drugs. Whatever she can get her hands on. Dan took me in when she disappeared on one of her binges, and he refused to give me back when she resurfaced. He was a cop at the time, so you can imagine how little leverage my mother had." She bit down on her lower lip. "Sometimes I think he paid her to go away, but he won't admit it."

Summer swallowed hard. "Wow." What did she say to that? Her life had been a picnic in comparison. "I'm sorry," she murmured.

"I got lucky having Dan look out for me, so it's all good. I try not to dwell on my mother."

For good reason, Summer thought.

Ava pushed back against the floor, rocking the

swing. "So how are you and Ben handling being secluded together?" Ava asked bluntly, changing the subject and taking Summer by surprise. "It can't be easy living under the same roof after everything. Although, like I said, it looks like you two are pretty cozy."

Summer blinked. Ava obviously knew something about her past with Ben. Had he told her everything? If so, it didn't paint Summer in the best light, but Ava was sitting here, opening up to her and expecting Summer to do the same.

She squirmed uncomfortably as she considered what to say. "Umm ... we're managing just fine." She didn't want to assume what Ava did and did not know, and inadvertently tell more than Ben wanted her to find out.

"Good. He looks at ease, and I'm glad. He's a good man, Summer. He doesn't deserve to be hurt."

"Is that directed at me?" Summer asked, suddenly defensive. "Because I've been nothing but up-front with him before and now." She bit the inside of her cheek and decided Ava pretty much knew everything about her shared past with Ben. "In fact, I did everything I could to try and let him keep his job. I wasn't the one who didn't return phone calls back then, so let's not throw around insinuations about who hurt who."

"You pass," Ava said. "You're defensive for yourself but you worried about Ben."

"You know, I don't appreciate being tested," Summer muttered.

Ava rolled her shoulders and leaned back against the swing. "That's what friends do. Look out for each other. I hope you'll forgive me."

Summer sighed. "I'm glad he has good friends." She had Ivy, but they were both always so busy it was hard to make time for quality get-togethers.

"Ben's a decent guy. He was there for me when I needed him, and I'll never forget that and always keep trying to repay the favor," Ava explained.

Summer crossed one leg over the other and looked up at the blue sky. "Given what I know about Ben, he wouldn't want repayment. He helped you because that's what he does for his friends."

"I appreciate that about him. But it's a two-way street." They sat in silence for a few minutes, then Ava spoke again.

"What's it like being a pop star? Singing in front of huge audiences?"

Summer gave the question some thought. "It's all I've ever known. When I was little, I sang at festivals, in chorus at school, in local plays. I love the performance aspect and the fact that I can feed off the energy of the crowd."

"I admire that. I can't carry a tune, and I'm much better off in the shadows," Ava said wistfully.

"Well, I admire what you do. Keeping people safe is no small feat."

"Would you give it up for any reason?" Ava asked.

Summer was surprised by the question. "It's all I've ever wanted. This opportunity to be the opening act for the biggest pop star in the world?" She shook her head. "I can't think of anything that would make me walk away."

"Not even for love?"

The question blindsided her, and Summer sat stunned that Ava would go there. Little did she know, Ben had put emotional attachment off-limits, and that was the smart way for her to think as well. She had no idea where her life was headed.

Before she could formulate a reply, the sliding glass door to the house opened and Ben appeared.

"Everything okay out here?" he asked.

Summer met his gaze, his blue eyes zeroing in on her as he stepped out into the fresh air. She drank him in, his white tee shirt lovingly clinging to muscles she'd held on to last night when he'd been deep inside her body.

No, they hadn't just slept together one night. Now that they were alone in the apartment, defensive barriers gone, at least as far as a sexual relationship was concerned, they made good use of their alone time. He'd switched from the pullout sofa into her bed, the move a natural transition they'd barely had to speak about or acknowledge.

Suddenly she couldn't tear her gaze away from his handsome face, Ava's question lingering in the back of her mind. Would she give up her dream for any reason? Including true love?

Not something she intended to think about. Not when her aspirations were finally within reach and the man in question wasn't interested in that kind of a relationship with her anyway.

AT FIRST BEN worried that Ava had been her usual overprotective self when it came to her friends and had alienated Summer, because ever since he'd interrupted their talk outside, Summer had been pensive and quiet. Then again, she'd been quiet since they arrived. But his friends were welcoming, Ava included, and as they day went on, Summer warmed up to them. He'd have hated for her to feel like she didn't belong and was glad she'd begun to come out of her shell.

What a contradiction she was, a vibrant star when it came to performing and a typical shy girl when in an intimate group of people she didn't know. He was a contradiction as well. On the one hand, he'd wanted to keep her separated from his friends and his life in order to better protect his heart; on the other hand, as he'd watched her today, he'd silently cheered when she had hit it off with the people who meant the most to him.

Dan grilled burgers, hot dogs, and corn on the cob. Ava had brought some sides, and the guys had come with store-bought desserts, everyone contributing. He wasn't surprised Ava had picked up a cake with candles for him, although he really could have lived without a big to-do. Turning thirty was enough for him to deal with. The brat hadn't bought candles with the numbers three and zero, no, she'd lined the entire cake with individual candles and made a production of lighting each one. The upside to the traditional birthday celebration had been Summer's gorgeous voice in tune and sounding over the guys' raspy attempts at singing.

Gifts came next, but he already knew Summer felt bad she didn't have one for him, and he downplayed the moment, glancing at his friends.

"How about I open them at home," he said, then realized he wouldn't be *home*, he'd be at Summer's apartment. In her bed, a place he was already itching to get back to.

He loved his friends and coworkers, but he was finished with the big group get-together and ready to get Summer naked and alone.

"He's ready to escape already," Dan said, chuckling. "Go ahead. I'm just glad you both came."

Tate laughed as well. "Hell, I'd want to get that pretty girl home safely and be alone, too." He winked at Ben, and Summer flushed a pretty pink.

Damned intrusive friends, Ben thought, still grateful for all of them. He hadn't heard from his father yet, which had become standard operating procedure. If he wasn't lost in a bottle, he was wasting his life away binge-watching shows. Anything not to live and feel again by risking his heart on another woman. Ben's mother hadn't been in his life for years.

When nobody else gave him a hard time, he and Summer said their good-byes and managed to slip out fairly quickly. They didn't talk much on the car ride home, the Uber driver a chatty guy who kept them occupied answering questions about things Ben couldn't even remember by the time they exited the vehicle.

They walked into the apartment, Summer humming, a sure sign that she'd enjoyed her day, and that fact made him too fucking happy.

She turned on the lights, then headed for the den, where he used to sleep, which wasn't too far a walk from her door. "Thank you for bringing me with you. It turned out to be fun," she said, tossing her purse onto the sofa.

"I'm glad you enjoyed. See? What did I tell you? Nobody bites."

She rolled her eyes at that, a cute smile lifting her lips.

"What about Ava?" he asked. "Did she overstep?" He placed his gift bags on the floor, an obvious bottle of alcohol sticking out from the top, definitely a gift from one of the guys. Ben flipped the lock, then the deadbolt, locking Summer in safely.

She ran her tongue over her bottom lip nervously and paused before answering. "Let's just say she was protective of you as her friend. But she didn't threaten to slit my throat, so I think we're good," she said wryly.

From her hesitancy, he knew she wasn't telling him everything, but her light way of handling it reassured him all really was fine with her and Ava's talk. He was willing to let it go. "Okay then. Sounds like you were able to handle her. I was worried."

"About me?" Summer asked, sounding surprised.

"Well, yeah. I didn't want Ava to say something that might send you running."

Summer made her way back toward him, her hips swaying as she walked. All day, he'd done his best not to focus on her body in that sexy dress, but it hadn't been easy. The pull of fabric at her waist showcased her fit form, her cleavage pushed up, two soft swells of flesh tempting him. And the teasing demure braid with tendrils of hair falling out had his mouth watering, visions of pulling on her hair as he pounded into her testing his restraint.

She kicked off her heels and aligned their bodies, his cock hard in his jeans, pressing against her stomach as she wrapped her arms around his neck. "Now why would I do that? I finally have you where I want you," she murmured. "There's no chance of me running anywhere but into your arms."

Her hands slid to the waistband of his jeans. She flicked open the button, unzipped his fly, and pushed the material down to the floor, taking his boxer briefs along with it. His cock sprung free, eager for whatever she had in mind next.

She always amazed him. In the moment, this was the same bold woman who had no trouble performing on stage. One who wasn't worried what anyone thought about her, only about what she wanted, and she clearly wanted him.

He had no trouble giving her what she desired.

Chapter Eight

AFTER PUSHING BEN'S pants to the floor, Summer dropped to her knees, wanting to taste him and give him the same pleasure he always gave her. She cupped his hard shaft in one hand and slid her tongue out, licking over the head, tasting his salty essence. Her own arousal grew, desire sweeping over her at the groan coming from deep inside him.

His hips jerked forward, his cock edging deeper into her mouth. Her eyes teared at the unexpected thrust, but she breathed through her nose and relaxed her muscles, only to have his entire body shudder as he hit the back of her throat.

"Fucking heaven," he growled, reaching down and wrapping her braid around his hand.

He tugged, her hair pulling away from her scalp, the feeling more erotic than painful, tingles shooting down her spine, moisture coating her panties. Maintaining her focus was difficult, but she intended to make him fall apart just like he so easily did to her.

She eased her mouth off, then pumped her hand up and down his shaft, teasing the head with her tongue before returning to sucking him in earnest. He began a steady pumping of his hips, his release obviously close.

She braced her hands on his thighs as the head of his cock hit the back of her throat with each pass, until she finally swallowed around him, causing him to fall over with a shout, his hot come spurting down her throat. She swallowed everything he gave, and only when he was done did she allow her knees to give way beneath her.

Ben didn't take long to catch his breath. He immediately picked her up and flung her over his shoulder, hauling her into the bedroom.

"Ben!" she shrieked at his possessive move but was laughing, too, until his hand came down on her ass in a light swat. "Hey! What are you doing?"

"I intend to repay the favor. We didn't stay long enough to eat dessert," he said as he toppled her onto the bed. He stripped off her dress, exposing her bra and panties, his blue eyes darkening with heat as he devoured her with his gaze.

He slipped a hand behind her and unhooked her bra with a deft move, then pulled the garment down her arms and off, tossing it to the floor before turning his attention to her panties.

"These have to go." He hooked his fingers into the sides and slid them off her legs, leaving her naked and bared to his hot stare.

To her shock, he was hard again and ready to go. As she stared at his thick, long cock, her sex swelled with need. "You have amazing stamina and recovery time," she whispered.

"It's you. I can't get enough." And to prove his point, he parted her slick folds, dipped his head, and began to eat the dessert he'd denied himself earlier.

Any witty reply she might have had died as his mouth began a slick, teasing tormenting of her flesh. He licked at the seam of her thigh and her sex, giving her a taste of what was to come. He lingered there before moving to the other side, and finally glided that talented tongue over her outer folds, pulling each one into his mouth, suckling hard before soothing with lighter laps of his tongue.

He played her well, bursts of desire alighting inside her, only to die out before she could climb higher. Her clit throbbed with need, but he deftly avoided touching her where she needed him most, denying her the orgasm her body craved.

She shifted her hips in a futile effort to control the pace, to urge him to touch her clit with his demanding tongue, but he remained determined to bring her to the brink and not allow her to fall over.

Her hips jerked up and she began to beg for relief. "Ben, please."

"Please what?"

"Make me come." She wasn't embarrassed to ask for what she needed, not when her body was on fire.

"How?" He flicked at her clit for the first time, not long or hard enough to give any real ease, but it allowed a hint of pleasure to surface once more. He nuzzled the tiny bud for longer this time before lifting his head. "What did you need, princess? I want to hear you say it."

"Suck me. Suck my clit. Make me come hard with your mouth, Please, Ben. No more teasing. I'm so on the—" Before she could finish her plea, he pulled her clit between his teeth and grazed her lightly before releasing her and continuing to lick over her with his tongue.

The unrelenting pressure was what she needed, and the glorious waves of her climax began to rush over her in never-ending waves. She came against his mouth, Ben taking her to the peak, letting her linger, and bringing her slowly down, playing her body perfectly.

She lay in a sated heap as Ben lifted himself up, his face coming over hers, kissing her so she tasted herself on his lips. "Ever had sex in the shower?" he asked, his throbbing erection pressing hard and insistent against her thigh.

She wouldn't have thought she was capable of being tempted again so soon, but this was Ben she was talking about. "Can't say that I have."

He chuckled and sat up. Next thing she knew, she was over his shoulder again and headed to her bathroom, where he settled her onto her feet.

"Be right back." He walked out and returned with a condom in hand, then turned the taps on, letting the water heat.

She took in the sleek lines of his back, the strong muscles and tapered waist and firm ass cheeks, biting the inside of her cheek as she admired the view.

She knew better. She really did, but she smacked his butt anyway.

He glanced over his shoulder, a heated warning in his eyes. "Looking for trouble?" he asked in a gruff voice.

She laughed. "I think I already found it."

He grinned and pulled back the curtain, picked her up, and placed her inside the tub, her feet gripping on the rubber mat as the warm water sluiced over her skin. He joined her, drawing the curtain and enclosing them inside.

He soaped his hands with her body wash and began to clean her skin, from her feet, up her calves, her knees, his big hands covering her thighs with foam. As he reached higher, he paused to tease her sex, gliding over her slick flesh, arousing her all over again.

Those hands continued up her stomach and over her breasts, pausing to play with her nipples, tweaking and pulling on the distended tips, every pinch sending shuddering flickers of desire throughout her body. After he was finished, he washed her hair, massaging her scalp with shampoo and rinsing with conditioner at her request or she'd never get the tangles out.

He moved her beneath the spray to clean off the soap before pushing back the curtain long enough to step away from the water and cover himself with the condom.

He turned her so her back was to the wall. "Hold on," he instructed, and she wound her hands around his neck as he lifted her, positioning her over his thick erection.

The head of his cock nudged at her entrance, and she moaned at the same time he joined their bodies, his cock parting her and sliding deep inside. The cool shower wall at her back contrasted with the heat they generated together as he thrust all the way home.

She closed her eyes, and as he let her adjust to his size, something she needed to do each time, her inner walls contracted around him, causing a trembling groan to escape from her throat.

"So hot," he said, gliding out and pumping back into her. "So wet." Another withdrawal and thrust of his hips. "So mine."

The words came out husky, and at the same moment, he began a hard, steady thrusting into her, taking them both over the edge almost immediately, her orgasm a living thing that devoured her body and took over her soul, all the while his words echoing inside her mind.

Mine. Mine. Mine.

His declaration wrapped around her as she came, and though she understood it was something he'd said in the heat of the moment, she knew she'd treasure it always. Even after he was gone.

As they reached Atlantic City, Summer bounced beside Ben, her excitement palpable. For all the places she'd performed as a child, new ones still brought a sense of giddy anticipation. On the approach, the hotels loomed in the distance, glittering signs welcoming them. The driver pulled up to the Borgata Hotel Casino and Spa, a tall building with black letters on top greeting them. Not even the prospect of seeing Tawny could dim her enthusiasm.

The lobby offered a sleek, clean, polished décor, with mirrored sculptures hanging from the ceiling and the sound of the nearby slot machines and ringing bells filling her ears.

They were checked in by a nice woman behind the front desk who was ultra-accommodating and informed Summer she'd been assigned a fifteen-hundred-square-foot suite. She wasn't used to the luxury and was still dumbstruck she wasn't in a regular room when she heard someone calling her name.

"Summer!"

She and Ben turned at the same time.

Michael strode up to her. "You're here!" He stepped in close, and Ben stiffened beside her.

"Hi, Michael."

"Hi. Anna asked me to look out for you because she couldn't be here."

Anna had touched base earlier, and Summer really didn't see the need for her agent to drop everything and travel to Atlantic City for one performance.

"Are we all set for tonight?" she asked Tawny's agent.

He straightened his suit jacket and nodded. "After you check in, you can look at our room. At four you'll need to be at the event center and go through a rehearsal. Tawny's due for a five o'clock run."

"Great!"

"Are you ready for tomorrow night?" He cast a worried glance her way. "Or are you still upset from the incident at Echo? Because everyone would understand if you're scared and wanted to drop out. Your safety is what matters most."

"What? No!" she said, horrified at the thought. "I never even considered dropping out."

Ben's strong hand came down on her shoulder. "She has no reason to be frightened. She has me to watch out for her," he said, giving her a reassuring squeeze. "All she has to focus on is performing."

Michael paused, as if evaluating her sincerity. Finally he nodded. "Okay, good. Then you're all set. I'll let you finish getting checked in. If you need anything, do you have my number?"

Summer nodded. Anna had given it to her just in case.

"Great. Then you know how to reach me." He patted his suit jacket, where the outline of his phone showed through.

"That was odd. I can't believe he thought I'd just give up," she said, glancing at Ben.

He frowned. "I don't like that guy," Ben muttered.

Summer didn't blame him. He often creeped her out with his invasion into her personal space.

"Let's get up to your suite and out of the open area," Ben suggested.

Knowing she'd have plenty of time to see the sights when they came down for rehearsal later, she agreed. Because the upside to leaving the large lobby was being alone with her bodyguard in that luxury suite.

★　★　★

AS BEN WATCHED, Summer studied the gray curved sofa in the center of the main room, the floor-to-ceiling windows behind it, the large king-size bed, and the double bath and Jacuzzi large enough for two, and sighed in delight. He saw extravagance in his line of work, protecting politicians and actors who came to the city, people who were used to the lap of luxury and took the things around them for granted. Her enjoyment of the ridiculously huge suite and the amenities provided for her by the hotel, courtesy of Jade Glow, was a joy to watch, and he hoped she never lost the sense of gratitude and awe that made her so special.

She stepped out of the bathroom she'd been ogling, a big grin on her face. "You know we have got to make use of that tub while we're here," she said, eyes twinkling with unmistakable desire and playfulness.

His cock twitched in his pants, almost as if asking him if they had time. He glanced at his watch. They'd left the city early and had hours before her rehearsal.

He shrugged and began to unbutton his shirt.

"Right now?" she asked, stepping up to him and

sliding his shirt off his shoulders, her soft fingertips grazing his skin.

He'd checked the lock when they arrived and now unhooked his holstered gun, planning to set it down beside him in the bedroom.

"I didn't see anything else on your agenda until later this afternoon." He grasped her around the waist, guiding her to the bedroom, where they made sizzling use of the king mattress, then lounged lazily in each other's arms in the huge tub. And Summer was nearly late for rehearsal.

After a flawless practice run, Ben surprised her with a reservation at a steakhouse owned by a famous television chef, telling himself that they had to eat. That it didn't mean anything special that he'd made the reservation and asked for a quiet table in the back, or that she'd been so happy he wasn't making her eat dinner in the hotel room that she'd almost had tears in her eyes and all he could think about was how he could put that glowing look on her face again soon.

Sure. Like the fact that he'd fallen into a routine, living with her as her boyfriend wasn't a big deal. He told himself he'd learned from his father's mistakes and he'd turned around and repeated his own, getting involved with a woman who, despite her best intentions—because Ben didn't think Summer was anything like his selfish mother—would take off and move on to bigger and better things. And he'd known the end result going in. Wasn't that why he'd insisted on great sex only? He had no business violating his own rules, but deep down, he knew he was.

By the time this assignment ended, she'd be ripping his heart out of his chest again, only this time it would be way worse because he was falling harder the more time they spent together. But that didn't mean he could take a rational, much needed step back.

He was in it for the painful duration.

THE NEXT NIGHT, even Ben had been able to tell Tawny's performance wasn't her best, while Summer's production and voice were spectacular. The other songstress's lack of energy and occasional off-key moments had been visible for all to see. Tawny didn't take the rough night well, throwing a tantrum behind the stage and storming out, presumably to her suite upstairs. Ben didn't envy her bodyguard or the people who surrounded her their jobs, dealing with a diva in the truest sense of the word. Even her agent didn't seem to have his usual calming effect on her.

Afterwards, they were taken to an exclusive part of the nightclub in the hotel, roped off for a party at which Summer was a guest. Ben lingered in the background, close enough to keep an eye on everyone and everything, including a good view of the only entrance to the elevated party area.

A waitress in a skimpy black cocktail dress offered Ben a drink, but he declined, instead cataloguing the servers, noticing they had specific women working this area of the club, making his job easier.

Tawny showed up late, but she obviously knew enough not to blow off such an important event. Photographers took pictures, and even Jade Glow made an appearance, spending time talking to both Summer and Tawny after having seen both women's performances.

Summer, dressed in a short sparkly red cocktail dress, beamed as she spoke to the major pop star, and the other woman was clearly impressed with Summer as well. His stomach cramped at the sight, knowing she was taking another step toward her dream, a huge positive for her, another nail in the coffin for them.

He scanned the crowd. Her agent, who'd managed to show up after all, and whom he'd met earlier, was schmoozing Jade Glow's agent. And once Jade herself had left, Tawny's bitchy attitude returned. Summer kept herself away from the other woman, talking to music executives who had come by as well.

An hour passed, and he hoped Summer would want to head upstairs soon. He wasn't a fan of the loud music or flashing club lights surrounding them.

Arms folded across his chest, he studied the area, stopping immediately as an unfamiliar woman wearing the black dress waitress uniform approached Summer with a drink on her tray.

Summer, he'd learned, wasn't a big fan of hard alcohol because it made her voice raspy. Wine was her choice. White wine, as she'd had with Ivy, or a glass of champagne, which was why the red-colored alcohol on the serving tray was a red flag, along with the fact that he didn't recognize the cocktail waitress carrying the drink and he'd been watching the same women for as long as they'd been at the club.

He didn't like how things were adding up in his mind, but someone unfamiliar handing her a drink she didn't normally prefer was odd. True, there was a better chance he was overreacting and the alcohol wasn't drugged, but he trusted his gut when it came to the job.

Summer glanced at the waitress and gave her a curious look before accepting the drink. Acting on instinct, Ben darted forward with every intention of stopping her from drinking, but a man in a suit stepped in front of him and he had to push him out of the way to get to her.

He wasn't in time to stop her from bringing the glass to her lips before he reached her and grabbed it out of her hand.

"Ben! What was that for?" she asked.

He grasped her elbow and pulled her aside, ignoring the stares of people around them. "Did you order this drink?" he asked.

"No. A waitress brought it over, and I was so thirsty. All this talking over the music," she explained.

He turned to look for the woman who'd served her, but she was gone.

"What's wrong?" Jack, Tawny's bodyguard, stepped up to them, grasping Tawny's arm and pulling her into their circle.

"Hey! What's with the manhandling? What's going on?" Tawny asked.

"I think someone drugged Summer's drink." Ben took a sniff but of course only inhaled the scent of red wine. "If it's GHB or Rohypnol, it won't smell. And according to recent studies, it gets lost in the color and fragrance of dark drinks." There was no way to test it.

"What the hell?" Jack turned to Tawny. "We're going up to the room. Immediately."

"The police will be questioning you," Ben warned the other woman.

She frowned his way but didn't reply. Instead she grew quiet and let Jack lead her away.

Ben needed to get Summer to her room, too, but they also needed to get this incident on record.

"I drank from it," she whispered in fear, her gaze

shooting to his.

"A lot?"

She shook her head. "A tiny sip before you stopped me." She looked up with gratitude in her gaze.

He slipped an arm around her waist and pulled her close. "You'll be okay. Even if I'm right and the drink was drugged, with the minute amount you ingested, you won't need the hospital." Although he could always take her there immediately if the need arose.

Just like after the trashing of her dressing area at the last event, he and Summer stayed for hours while the police came and took their statements. They agreed to test the drink, although they concurred with Ben's assessment that there was very little chance of anything showing up. And they wrote down Tawny's name and promised to question her and her entourage, especially since she'd been missing from the area for a long while.

The good news was that if Summer had finished the drink or taken enough to poison her system, she'd be showing signs of the drug, but she was coherent, just exhausted.

Meanwhile Ben requested the manager let them view security video, because Ben would recognize the unfamiliar waitress who'd suddenly shown up to serve Summer, and if there was a chance the woman had met with Tawny, maybe they'd see it. As it was an

Atlantic City casino hotel, security cameras were everywhere, even on the bar.

Summer sat in a chair in front of the cameras, Ben behind her, leaning over to observe the screen in front of them. It didn't take long to isolate the thirty minutes before Summer had been served.

He scanned the crowded bar on the screen, quickly zeroing in on the woman with blonde hair, wearing a black cocktail dress, sitting at the bar. "That's her."

The security guard who was running the video paused and pulled a close-up of her face. "You're sure?"

Ben nodded. "I am."

"I don't understand," Summer murmured.

He squeezed her shoulder. "Run the video."

The woman ordered a drink, and sure enough, the bartender passed her a glass of red wine.

"I don't recognize her," the manager, who was also watching carefully, said. "She's not one of ours."

"Yet she walked to the side of the bar, picked up a serving tray, and mingled through the crowd, into the roped-off area, and handed Summer a drink," Ben said through clenched teeth.

The woman then turned away from the bar, unknowingly facing the camera as she eased her hand into her apron pocket and slipped something into Summer's drink. No Tawny or evidence of who'd paid the woman to drug Summer.

"Fuck!" Ben turned angrily toward the manager. "Well?"

"What can I say?" Red-faced, the man straightened his shoulders in self-defense. "The place is a zoo on a good night. I wasn't given a heads-up to tighten security."

"Make sure the police get a copy," Ben instructed the man.

But that wasn't enough. He intended to make sure Jade Glow's agency took this situation more seriously. They needed to hire someone to figure out who was after Summer and why. Ben's job, his sole priority, was to get Summer to a safe location and keep her there.

BACK IN THE room, Summer couldn't relax. She paced the floor while Ben spoke to his boss, demanding they put someone on Tawny's tail and bill it to the people covering Summer's protection. Threats were one thing, he said. Escalating was something else, and *she could have fucking died thanks to an overdose.* He was furious and angry on her behalf, but his words merely drove home everything that had happened tonight.

Shaking, she left him on the phone and headed for the bedroom area, unnerved by the fact that someone had tried to drug her. Scared about how close she'd come to drinking the poison. During the night's investigation, she'd sat in silence, feeling dizzy. She'd thought.

But she hadn't said anything because she assumed she was just reacting to the power of suggestion and fear. She really had taken such a small sip, she finally accepted the fact that she was going to be fine, which left her time to think. About those moments after Ben had saved her from drinking the alcohol and while he'd been trying to find out whether she'd been drugged.

She'd sat in the security room, Ben's sole focus on the screens in front of him, and one painful fact had been driven home to her—she was alone. Her best friend couldn't give up her career to follow Summer around, and her parents had abandoned her, hurt feelings more important than family ties. In her career-driven life, she'd never had time to make a group of friends, and in her profession, people were more competitors like Tawny than gal pals. At least the people she'd met so far. And Ben was pretty sure at this point Tawny was involved, which made Summer sick to her stomach.

She heard Ben's voice from the other room as he talked on the phone. And what about Ben? He was her bodyguard … for now. Her protector. But he'd be gone when his assignment ended. With a lump in her throat, she washed up and finally climbed into bed, her heart still racing inside her chest, fear mixed with raw pain.

He came in soon after, climbing in beside her. She hadn't realized how many emotions she'd been holding in until he pulled her into his arms and she burst into tears.

"Hey. Everything's going to be fine," he said, pulling her close and running a hand over the back of her hair.

She took a shuddering breath, grateful for his strength and support. "I know. I just…"

"Talk to me. You've been through a lot in a short time. You've got the stress of the competition, the performances, someone sabotaged your dressing area, now you were almost drugged."

"Explain why someone would want to do this to me? Even Tawny. That drug could have done serious damage, and for what? A leg up on me? What was she thinking?"

"At the very least, you would have acted without inhibitions. Maybe she was hoping to catch you on camera doing something outrageous. Something that would get you kicked out of the running to open for Jade. She's certainly played that card before."

Summer swallowed hard. "God, I hate to admit it, but that makes sense, especially if the tape went viral, like the one did back on *Star Power.*"

"There's something else that's been bugging me," Ben said.

"What's that?"

"Michael Gold. He's always around, quietly in the background. My gut churns when he's in the area."

Summer thought about his words, weighing possibilities in her mind. "I'm all for looking into every angle, and he is in Camp Tawny … but he's a professional."

Ben shrugged. "I'm not discounting him. I'll have Dan add him to the list of people to look into."

"Okay."

"Are *you?* Okay?" He stroked her arm in a soothing motion. "Like I said, it's been a lot for you to handle."

She sniffed, the earlier emotions returning at the reminder. "It's a lot for someone alone to handle."

He stiffened beside her, then those big, strong arms squeezed her tighter. "You are not alone."

Tears leaked out of her eyes because he couldn't be more wrong. "I miss my family. For most of my life, I had their support, and now, when I need them to be my parents, not my managers, they're nowhere to be found."

He rolled her to her back, pushing himself up on one arm so he could meet her gaze. "Maybe you need to tell them."

"I can't get them on the phone or video chat long enough to explain what's going on."

He leaned down and brushed his lips over hers. "They'd care if they knew. I believe that."

Deep down, she agreed. "I do, too." It just wasn't easy to break the ice or get them to really hear her these days. "I'll try," she murmured.

"Good."

He pulled her into him. "Get some sleep and we'll get out of here early tomorrow. Put this whole nightmare behind you."

She nodded and allowed her heavy lids to close, breathing in the comforting smell of Ben in her bed. Her breathing evened out, and just as she felt herself drift, she heard him speak.

"You aren't alone," he said, stroking her arm. "You have me."

It was low. It was quiet. For the moment, it was everything.

Chapter Nine

B EN WAS GRATEFUL to get Summer back home to her quiet New York City apartment, away from the hustle of Atlantic City and the fear that followed her there. At least here he had a semblance of control. The main reason someone had been able to get to her was because they knew her public schedule. But as long as they were holed up in her apartment, she was safe.

His new plan included varying her gym routine, switching up her days. He insisted Ivy take alternate routes over, as she was a direct link to Summer. Anything to throw Tawny or whoever was behind this off Summer's tail.

Ben still believed Tawny was behind the incidents. Whether her agent had a hand in it or not remained to be seen, too. He'd called Dan and added Michael Gold to the suspect list of people he wanted looked into. At least he felt he'd done everything he could think of for now, when it came to keeping Summer safe.

He double-checked the locks on the apartment for the night while Summer showered. He was looking forward to crawling into bed and losing himself in the warmth and heat of her body. His dick perked up in agreement.

His cell rang and he pulled it from his pocket. At a glance, he didn't recognize the number but he answered anyway. "Hollander."

"Ben?" his father asked in a rough voice.

Ben's gut clenched at the familiar voice. "Dad? Where are you calling from?" Ben asked, concerned because he only heard from his father when something was wrong. A problem with his health or a self-pitying rant.

"Umm. About that. You see, I have a problem. I was arrested and I need you to post bail."

"What?" he shouted into the phone, prompting Summer to rush out of the bathroom, wrapped in a towel.

"What happened? What's wrong?" she asked, her eyes wide and full of worry.

Ben gripped his phone tighter, disgust and embarrassment running through him. He held up a hand, tearing his gaze from the sight of her long, wet hair falling over her shoulders and her breasts plumping up over the edge of the towel.

"Arrested for what, Dad?" he asked through gritted teeth.

Summer gasped but Ben was focused on the voice on the phone. Given his father's weaknesses, he was afraid the situation involved alcohol. Luckily until now, his dad hadn't hurt anyone else while abusing liquor, but Ben had been called from bars when his father's credit card was denied and he'd needed cash to close out his account.

Silence followed his question before Nate finally replied.

"Drunk driving," came the muffled reply. "I need you to post bail."

Ben ran a hand over his face, anger, humiliation and frustration warring inside him. Why couldn't his father deal with his shit like a man? An adult who could bounce back from adversity?

"Where are you exactly?" he asked, gesturing for Summer to find him a pen and paper.

She ducked into her room and returned with a pink pad and a pen, which he used to write down the jail nearest his father's house in Hewlett, which was a solid hour and a half from Summer's apartment, no traffic.

"Got it. I'll be there in the morning."

"But…"

Ben shook his head, refusing to give in to guilt for

not rushing to bail him out now. "By the time I show up, they won't process you out anyway." He wanted his father sober when he saw him, plus a night in jail to think about how dangerous his actions had been might help.

"Time's up!" a loud voice called out, obviously letting his father know he had to hang up the phone.

"I've gotta go. Thanks, son." He disconnected the call, and Ben cringed knowing he had no choice but to turn and face Summer. The explanation he'd been avoiding giving her, the truth about his father, his parents, his background, was about to come out.

"Ben? Is your father okay?" Summer asked gently.

He shrugged his shoulders, not knowing the answer to that question. It ought to bother him more, but he was so tired of seeing his father drunk or hungover, which was why these days he barely saw him at all.

"He's probably sobering up and coming to terms with being picked up for a DWI," he muttered.

She tucked the towel tighter around her. "And is this an unusual thing? Him being drunk? And driving?"

He swallowed hard. "Why don't you go get dressed and I'll explain after." He needed a minute to gather his thoughts and pull his composure further around him.

She nodded, spun around, and headed for the bedroom.

He gave her a few minutes to change while he stared out the window over the glittering city lights. Ben wasn't a jerk. He understood his father had a serious issue. He'd just feel better about it if the man were willing to get himself some help instead of spending all these years indulging past pain.

He heard the sound of a drawer close in the bedroom and knew he couldn't stall any longer. He headed to join Summer.

She sat on top of the bed wearing an oversized white tee shirt, her nipples poking through the fabric, her legs drawn up to her chin, a sexy peek of her panties visible.

He ignored the unintentional view for the more serious conversation they were going to have and settled on the edge of the bed. "I mentioned I don't celebrate my birthday … unless forced."

"You did allude to something like that." She waited patiently, those big brown eyes softening as they focused on him.

He thought back to when he was little. "I remember parties when I was little." One party in particular, with streamers in the garage and a magic show. "My mom and dad would both be there. But after things fell apart, I don't remember any holidays or happy celebrations." He didn't feel sorry for himself, he was just ... resigned to how things were. How they had been for the last twenty years.

He glanced at Summer, who waited patiently, as if sensing he needed to tell this story on his own time, at his own pace.

Ben knew it would never get easier, so he dove in. "My dad and his best friend, Tom, were partners in a lucrative import-export business, and Mom worked there, too, handling the books. Tom Milford wasn't married and he spent holidays with my family. To me he was my uncle, as much family as if he were blood related." Ben remembered looking up to the big bear of a man, as much as he once had to his father, which was why the betrayal hurt badly.

"The business began to expand quickly, and it was my father who did the overseas travel to procure items for shipment and to handle contracts with the overseas companies. And he was good at what he did." He swallowed hard. "To sum up an ugly story, my mother and my uncle had an affair. I was sleeping at a friend's. Dad came home early from a business trip and caught them in bed."

He winced as he said the words, unable to imagine how betrayed his father must have felt. Which was why Ben's frustration with the man made him feel so conflicted. Did he feel sorry for him? Was he angry with him for not getting over it? It was a difficult mixture of both.

"Ouch." Summer sunk her teeth into her bottom lip. "How old were you?" she asked.

"Ten when the marriage began to unravel. Apparently when she was caught, my mother got hysterical. She cried and said it was a mistake, that they were both sorry… She begged my father to take her back and he did."

"So he forgave them. That shows strength of character," Summer said.

"I once thought so. Maybe it did … then. The problem was, they did it again. Or maybe they never stopped. Dad was wary at first but things seemed okay. He became complacent and they carried on behind his back." Ben groaned, rubbing a hand along the back of his neck, working out the tension there. He hated thinking of the past, his mother's behavior and lack of caring for anyone but herself.

"What happened? How did he find out the second time? Did your dad catch them again?" she asked.

Ben nodded, nauseated over what came next. "In the office, a year later, and this time, Mom didn't beg him to take her back. She announced she was leaving him for Tom. Which meant Dad had a choice. He could walk away, be bought out according to the partnership agreement, and leave the business he'd built or come to work every day and face them. Together."

"He opted for the buyout?" Summer guessed.

"He did. He put the money in the bank and wallowed in self-pity. That's when the drinking began. Of course, I didn't find out all the details until I was older. And after Dad began to drink … and ramble and admit the sad family truths."

"And your mother? What happened?"

"She and Tom married. Had kids of their own." His stomach cramped at the reminder of the parent he no longer had. He thought he'd come to terms with it, but repeating the story now fucking hurt. "I wanted nothing to do with them then, and it hasn't changed now. Because she let Dad raise me. She didn't bother with me, signed over full custody because she couldn't deal with the friction with Dad."

Summer held out her arms, and despite not wanting pity for his pathetic childhood, he climbed beside her. She laid her head against his chest in a gesture of comfort.

"Was he a good father?" she asked.

"He was physically present," Ben said. "That's the best I can say. I had food on the table and a parent at home because he was too depressed to find a job or try to create a new business. While I lived at home, he tried, a little, to be there."

But Ben had seen him withdraw into himself, to decline over the years until he was no longer the man he'd once been. "What I took away from watching my father was to never repeat my mistakes. Taking her back was a huge error in judgment. He wanted to believe the marriage he had was real, but he'd obviously missed something key in their relationship, because she betrayed him a second time."

"That's sad," she murmured. "I'm sorry. It explains why you were so hesitant to get involved with me again."

His smile was grim. "I learned not to trust in much," he admitted. "Add to that I was just hurt and angry at myself that I was stupid enough to violate my contract and lose my job."

"Stupid enough to get involved with me?" she asked, smiling despite the conversation.

"I couldn't resist you, Summer. Then or now."

Her face lit up at his words. And since he'd have to deal with the fallout of his father's actions tomorrow, tonight he wanted to get lost in Summer's arms.

WHEN BEN TURNED toward her, Summer could read the need in his eyes. Desire was there, but so was the yearning to get lost and replace his pain with something else. Something she could provide.

She sat up on her knees and lifted his shirt, pausing to glide her palms up the light coating of hair on his chest and over his nipples, scratching with her nails before she eased the shirt over his head and tossed it onto the floor. She took in his muscled forearms and pecs, his tanned skin, and leaned down for a taste.

She followed the reverse path with her mouth, gliding her lips over his chest, teasing his nipples with her tongue and teeth before licking her way down to the waistband of his shorts.

He gripped her breasts in his hands as she moved, tweaking her nipples, moisture flooding her underwear, desire rushing through her. With his help, they removed his pants and boxer briefs, his cock huge and erect, his naked body hers to explore.

The problem was, he obviously didn't want slow, because he ripped her panties off with a swift tug and lifted her, positioning her over his straining shaft. Her legs quivered, barely holding her up, the feel of his pulsing heat between her thighs a heady thing.

She was gone for him but not so far gone that she wasn't aware of the situation. At least not yet. "Condom," she managed to croak out, not easily with her body softening and demanding to be filled by his thick erection.

"At least someone's thinking," he said with a shake of his head.

She held herself up on her knees, waited while he leaned over and pulled a packet from the nightstand drawer, where they'd stashed their supply, and covered himself with the condom.

He quickly returned his hands to her hips, lifting her up and placing her over his hard cock once more. She slid down a tiny bit, a tease of sorts, clenching him tight inside her, feeling him as he parted her slick heat.

His big body reverberated, and he groaned aloud, a sexy sound of torment she enjoyed, and she took him in a little more. And a little more, deliberately torturing him with a slow dance of seduction, at least the slowest she could manage with the flutters of desire beating inside her, growing larger the more of him she took into her body. He gripped her hips, his fingertips digging ever harder into her skin until she was sure he'd leave marks.

Unable to take it any longer, she released her grip on his shaft and slid down hard on top of him, accepting his thick length inside her completely.

"Ride me," he said in a gritty voice.

"With pleasure." She grasped his hands in hers, holding on as she began to slide up and down, a steady beat that allowed him to thrust into her over and over, each pass ending with a grind of her sex against his pelvis. Every press of their bodies causing a shock of pleasure to rush over her, stronger each time.

It was fast, it was furious, the pounding of his body up and into hers, and her climax hit almost immediately in a sudden burst of sensation, her orgasm rushing over her in waves that continued as he began to pump upward, causing her to come harder and longer, as he, too, found release with a loud shout.

His hips grinded into her body, his thickness swelling inside her, and she came again on a sob, collapsing on top of him, his arms bracketing her in warmth.

SUMMER WOKE UP to the sunlight streaming through the slatted shades, worried about Ben and the day ahead. He rolled over, coming to consciousness slowly, his heavy-lidded stare focusing on her.

"Morning," he said gruffly in his sexy, sleep-roughened voice.

"Good morning." She lay on her side and met his gaze.

"Listen, don't worry about being alone today. I'll get someone over here to look out for you before I go bail out my father." He pushed himself up in the bed and leaned against the headboard. "If I can't get someone from Alpha Security, Dan will call in a favor and get a person he trusts from another company to take over."

"What?" She eased herself into a sitting position as

well, pulling the covers up and over her bared breasts. "No. I'm coming with you."

He frowned at her words. "I am not taking you to a county jail. And I'm sure as hell not exposing you to my father after a night in a cell." He wrinkled his nose in disgust. "I'm your bodyguard and my job is to keep you safe."

"Oh, cut the crap," she muttered, knowing excuses when she heard them. He was obviously embarrassed by the situation and he didn't want her there, but tough luck.

"What the hell does that mean?"

"We might not have a label on what's happening between us…" And he might want it to be about sex… "But it's more than just you're my bodyguard." She reached out and gently stroked his cheek, letting her touch linger. "I … care about you, and I'm going to be beside you when you deal with your dad and his situation."

His mulish expression hadn't changed, but she ignored it just as she planned to ignore any argument he formed. "I'll take a fast shower and be ready to go when you are," she said, rising from the bed.

"Do I have a choice?" he asked in a grumpy tone.

She shook her head. She wasn't taking no for an answer. Which was why she found herself beside Ben in an Uber to his apartment, so he could grab his car keys and drive them in his SUV to pick up his father.

Ben was silent on the way there, and she didn't press him to talk, just grateful he hadn't found a way to leave her behind. She'd meant what she said. They might not have a defined relationship, but she more than cared about him and she knew it. She had a feeling he did, too, but he hadn't indicated he felt any more for her than convenient, easy sex buddies while they were together. Their chemistry was off the charts. It always had been.

But today wasn't about sex. Today was about being there for him in ways that mattered.

★   ★   ★

HIS FATHER REEKED of alcohol and disgusting jail cell odors Ben would prefer not to identify when he finally bailed him out and loaded him into the back seat of his car. Nate was sullen and morose, introductions between Summer and his dad not going all that well. Nate grated out a hello, while Summer's cheery disposition had no effect on his father's mood.

What an embarrassing clusterfuck. Of all the times for his father to get arrested for drunk driving, it had to be while Ben was on an assignment he couldn't separate himself from.

He recalled Summer's words from earlier this morning. *We might not have a label on what's happening between us, but it's more than just you're my bodyguard.* He swallowed hard. At least one of them was being honest. She wasn't here because he was her security detail. She was here because they had a relationship, undefined though it might be.

After today, who knew what their status would be. If Summer was smart, after a day with Nate Hollander, she'd run the other way, far and fast. The thought made him ill. He'd come to terms with the fact that he wanted as much time with Summer as he could get before life pulled them in separate directions.

He turned into his father's driveway and shut off the engine, the three of them trudging into the house. The ranch hadn't changed, nor had his father done much in the way of upkeep. The house was a dump and heaped more embarrassment on Ben's shoulders in front of Summer for the way his dad lived.

But, he reminded himself, if Nate didn't want help, he couldn't force him to get it. He'd be laying down the law later, and his father would have to make some hard choices. Because Ben wouldn't be bailing him out ever again.

"I need a shower," his father muttered, heading for the master bedroom in the back of the house.

Ben let him go. He needed his father cleaned up for what he had to say next.

"Is there food in the refrigerator?" Summer asked,

standing in the family room. "I can make something to eat for when he's finished."

"I don't know. And you don't have to wait on him." He didn't mean to sound ungrateful. This whole situation had him on edge.

"I know I don't have to. I want to." Summer headed for the kitchen. "He'll feel better after he gets something in his stomach." She opened the refrigerator, and Ben groaned at the sight that greeted her.

Old takeout leftovers sat inside, and beer lined the door shelves.

"What if I go pick up some fresh food at the grocery store?" she offered. "Oh, wait! There are eggs in here. And bread," she said, reaching into the back of the fridge. She glanced at both, studying dates. "And they're not expired!" She sounded like she'd hit the lottery.

At least his father had enough food in the house for a meal and a supermarket run wasn't also on today's agenda. Because even though they were far from the city, Ben wasn't leaving Summer alone.

"I'm really grateful you're offering, but you don't need to cook for him," he tried again.

"He needs protein," she insisted, and began to search the kitchen for plates, silverware, and a frying pan, lining the counter with the items she needed, her ponytail bouncing behind her.

Summer got to work and Ben headed to deal with his father, pausing in the entry to the kitchen and turning around. She hummed while she busied herself, first cleaning up the dishes in the sink and loading the dishwasher before getting to work.

"Summer…"

She glanced over her shoulder, those big eyes meeting his.

He meant to say thank you. To somehow find a way to express his gratitude, but the words wouldn't come. Instead he stalked back into the room and pulled her into his arms, his embrace hopefully communicating what he wasn't able to say.

Just the fact that she was here, that she'd insisted on joining him when she could have waited at home, said something about the depth of the relationship they had and chose not to discuss.

"You're a special woman, Summer. I really didn't want to do this alone," he finally admitted, kissing the top of her head.

"I want to be here for you."

He warned himself to ignore not just the fragrant scent that enveloped him but the twisting of his heart at her words. Words he wished she meant for a lot longer than this one crisis.

"Ben!"

His father's call interrupted his wayward thoughts.

"Coming, Dad!"

She stepped back and gave him a reassuring smile. "I'll get his breakfast going. Want anything?" she asked.

He shook his head. "No thanks. I'm not hungry." Not for food, anyway.

He was hungry for Summer. All of her and not just sex. Her support today made him realize how much he longed for more than she was able to give. They could be a good team … if the world stage wasn't waiting.

SUMMER FINISHED COOKING breakfast for Ben's father, which he devoured in less than two minutes flat. Scrambled eggs and toast. That was about all she could manage for him, but he hadn't seemed to care what was on the plate. She didn't know if Nate was hungover or just starving after his night in jail, but he grunted about how good the food was as he ate.

She covertly studied him, her gaze going from Nate to Ben and back again. Although Nate's skin was sallow and his face drawn, Summer saw traces of his son in his features. He had probably been a handsome man years ago, before he'd let life beat him down. She swallowed over the lump in her throat, trying not to let her emotions overwhelm her. Ben had enough to deal with without her getting upset on his behalf.

He waited for his father to finish eating before turning a kitchen chair around and straddling the back, facing the older man. "Dad, we need to talk."

Summer took that as her cue. "I'll go into the other room," she said. She could finish the dishes later.

"No." Ben met her gaze, imploring her with his eyes. "Stay. Please."

She nodded and picked up his father's plate, carrying it over to the sink before leaning against the counter and waiting. She didn't know where this conversation would be going, and her heart beat hard inside her chest.

"Dad, here's the situation," Ben began. "This was a one-shot deal. I won't be bailing you out again. If you get arrested, you're on your own."

His father's shoulders hunched over, his posture defeated. "It's never happened before."

Ben set his jaw, his shoulders tense and straight. "And it can't happen again. Either you get yourself help—real help—or I won't be answering the phone when you need a bar tab paid or God forbid you kill someone driving drunk." Ben's face flushed red as he spoke, and she knew, without a doubt, how difficult this was for him.

She hadn't wanted to embarrass Nate Hollander by staying and listening to whatever it was Ben intended to say, but she now realized that was part of his plan.

Shock, embarrass, and hopefully get his father to hear him and finally get help for his problem.

Ben was a good, decent man, and he wouldn't want to abandon his father in his time of need, but it was obvious, both from the run-down condition of the house and Nate's lack of caring about much of anything, that Ben had no choice.

"I don't know if I can stop." Nate stared at his hands clutched tightly together.

Ben's gaze narrowed. "You mean you don't know if you want to. It's not going to be easy, Dad, but I'll support you as long as you're trying."

The silence in the wake of Ben's statement was deafening, Summer thought.

"I have a friend who goes to AA." Nate finally spoke up. "Maybe I could call him." He glanced up at his son, as if asking whether that was enough of a concession.

"That's a start. But you have to want to sober up. You need to face your problems and your life. You want to do that? I'll be there." He tipped his head toward Summer. "You ready?" he asked, obviously not expecting a definitive answer from his father right now ... or miracles after dropping his ultimatum.

"I, umm, I wanted to wash the dirty dishes." She gestured to the pan and plate she'd left in the sink.

Ben shook his head. "You already cleaned up his

mess. He can handle this one," he said in a firm voice that told her he wouldn't accept any argument.

"Okay." She walked toward where Ben stood in the kitchen entrance, pausing by his father at the table. "It was nice to meet you, Mr. Hollander. I hope you feel better soon."

He lifted his head. "Thank you, Summer. I appreciate your help."

It was the first acknowledgment he'd given her, and she smiled before letting Ben lead her out of the house and back to his car.

She waited until they were settled and on the way back to Manhattan before she spoke. "That was strong, the way you handled him."

"I feel like shit," he said, his words honest and raw.

"Of course you do." She reached over and grabbed his hand, holding on tight. He could drive with his free hand. "But you had no choice. You can't enable him and you're right. The next time, he could kill or hurt someone ... or himself."

"I hope he realizes that himself."

She lifted his hand and pressed a kiss to his skin. "You did the best you could."

"I wish to God you didn't have to see him like that," he said.

"I don't judge you based on your father," she said. "I'm just glad I could be there for you."

"I wish you always could be." She knew the words had slipped out, the emotions of the day at the surface for Ben.

And her eyes filled with tears because he'd never know how much she wished the same thing.

Chapter Ten

SUMMER WAS FOLDING clothes in her room, having done laundry, and Ben sat on the couch, checking work email on his laptop. He'd had a few peaceful days with no stress from Summer's schedule and no word from his father. He hadn't expected to hear from Nate, and he wasn't of the mindset that no news was good news, because his silence could just as easily mean he'd gone back to his drinking rather than make an attempt to sober up. Time would tell.

As for Summer, she didn't have another engagement planned until a media junket over the following weekend. According to her agent, Jade's tour opened in a little over two months and she was getting closer to making a decision. As much as Ben wanted Summer's dreams to come true, he wasn't looking forward to the end of this assignment. The end of them. He hadn't listened to his gut or his own words to Summer, and kept his distance.

He'd introduced her to his friends and colleagues and brought her into his fractured family life. She knew him better than even those at Alpha Security who were closest to him. And she'd supported him in ways that he'd never let anyone else do.

He'd allowed her to see the weakest part of him, and instead of running away, she'd stepped up. Hell, she'd cooked for his old man. She'd been quiet when he needed silence to process the day, and open and giving when he'd needed her later that night.

And *he* knew *her*. From her hopes and dreams of success to her endearing insecurities before going on stage, he understood her. He wanted to protect the girl who'd been hurt by her parents from further pain, and at the same time he wished he could shake them and make them be there for her when she needed them.

This was the closest he'd let himself get to any woman in his life, and losing her was going to rip his heart out because he'd fallen in love with her.

He'd been too wrapped up in his anger with his father to see it then, but looking back, he'd known it the second he'd seen her making eggs for his hungover dad. Ponytail bouncing against her back, no judgment in her gaze, she was his perfect woman. No matter how big a star she became, he loved the normal girl she was inside.

And fuck. That thought ripped through him painfully, because there was no happy ending that he could see. The upcoming feeding frenzy with the press junket might be the last event before her life's direction took a drastic change. He refused to consider that she wouldn't get the opportunity she deserved, because he didn't want to be with her only because she'd lost her big chance. She'd never be happy that way. Not even with him by her side.

He ran a hand through his hair and groaned just as an email popped up on his screen from Dan. He opened the note from his boss and read: *No luck with Tawny Renee situation. From all indications, she's absorbed in her own opportunities. Even her bodyguard interview came up empty. He thinks she's innocent of all wrongdoing against Summer. Still watching her though.*

As for Michael Gold, the man was a piece of work. He'd married into money and had gotten his start thanks to his father-in-law being in the talent industry. And his wife, with whom he had three children, was a brilliant entertainment lawyer. He'd been treading water as an agent before he'd gone to work for his father-in-law, owing everything to the older man. Or so it seemed. So he was greedy and a slimy asshole, but nothing stood out on him, either, in Dan's report. Which meant until whoever was after Summer made a mistake, they were shit out of luck.

Summer walked out of her room, wearing a pair of

ripped leggings and an oversized sleep shirt. Makeup-free, she looked even younger and so beautiful.

"Hey." She treated him to a wide smile.

"Hey yourself," he said.

"So I was thinking," she said as she rocked back and forth on the balls of her feet, clearly wired.

"What's up?"

"I need a change of scenery. I want to get away from these walls that feel like they're closing in on me."

He narrowed his gaze, his focus on her safety, as always. "What did you have in mind?"

"Well…" Her eyes glimmered with excitement. "When we were driving out to your father's, I saw a carnival off one of the exits. The Ferris wheel was in the distance. And it was closer rather than farther from the city, and I want to go." She settled in next to him on the sofa and nudged his arm. "And before you argue, it's spur of the moment, so nobody will know we're going except us. It's perfectly safe." She folded her arms across her chest and met his gaze, all but daring him to argue.

He tossed around the idea in his mind. Crowds of people, yes, but she had a point when she said nobody would know where they were going in order to follow them.

"A carnival, hmm?" he asked, deliberately dragging

out his decision, teasing her a little.

She nodded. "The kind with cotton candy, funnel cake, rides, and games where you can win me a stuffed animal. Come on, please? Please? Pretty please," she said, a grin on her pretty face as she tried to pester him into agreeing.

Having just accepted his feelings for her, there was very little he wouldn't give her while he could ... as long as she was safe.

He groaned, pretending to be put out at the idea ... more teasing on his end before giving in.

"Pretty please with sugar on top?"

He laughed, then nodded his head in agreement. "Fine. We'll go."

"Wait. What? Really? Thank you!" She squealed in excitement and clapped her hands with glee before leaning in and kissing him hard but quickly.

Too quickly, considering he'd rather pull her down on the sofa and find himself balls deep in her wet heat.

"I'm going to change!"

She ran into her room, and while she was there, he catalogued his own clothes, deciding his jeans and a tee shirt would be fine. He holstered his gun beneath the shirt just as she bounced back out to him, this time wearing a pair of light jeans, a faded gray tee shirt, and sneakers, a pair of aviator glasses dangling from her fingertips.

He grinned at the sight. "Wait. I have an idea." He strode to his duffel in her room and returned with a New York Mets ball cap, plunking it down on her head, tugging on her braid for good measure. "There. We want you as disguised as possible."

"Not that I think anyone will recognize me but okay." She patted the brim of the hat, her big eyes peeking out from beneath.

She wrinkled her nose, her expression fucking cute.

"Mark my words, no one will recognize me. Today we're just a normal couple out for a day of fun."

And he intended to savor every last second.

SUMMER WAS HAVING a blast. She couldn't recall the last time she'd gone to a carnival or festival for the pure fun of it, not to perform and entertain. The day was warm, the sun overhead as she and Ben walked around the site, arm in arm. Wanting to take advantage of her time here, she coaxed him on every ride imaginable, from the Ferris wheel she'd seem from the highway to the other rides like the Round Up and Scrambler, to the more sedate carousel.

Ben was a great sport, not once complaining about the type of ride she'd cajoled him onto or all the junk food she ate. Their current stop was the cotton candy stand, where she watched a woman turn spun sugar into a coated sticky delicious treat.

Ben hadn't let her pay for a thing, so after he'd taken care of buying her latest indulgence, they walked to an empty bench and took a seat. She scooped a finger full of candy and held it out for him to taste.

His heavy-lidded eyes met hers as he grasped her wrist, lifted her hand, and swirled his tongue around the soft, sugary treat, pulling her finger into his mouth and biting down on the tip. An electric jolt traveled straight to her sex, and she was unable to control the low moan that escaped her throat, her nipples tightening, moisture pooling between her thighs.

"You're a bad girl," he said in a husky voice, his gaze hot on hers.

She grinned in reply. "You started it."

"I'd finish it, too, if we weren't sitting in a public place."

She squirmed in her seat, her sex damp and desire flooding through her.

"Excuse me." Two young girls walked over, interrupting them.

"Yes?" Ben asked.

"Hi," Summer said, using a tone warmer than her bodyguard had.

"Umm, aren't you Summer Michelle? I saw you on *The Morning Show.*"

She pursed her lips in thought. A part of her wanted to give the girls what they wanted, but this was her day out with Ben. She'd assured him they were safe, and she intended to keep them that way.

"No, I'm not. But you're not the first people to think that," she said, trying to lighten their obvious disappointment. They'd been hoping for a mini-celebrity sighting.

"Okay, well, sorry to have bothered you," the other girl said. She nudged her friend as they walked away. "I told you it wasn't her! You're so ridiculous." Giggling, they headed off toward one of the rides.

Summer glanced up at Ben. "See? We're just a normal couple out for a day at the carnival," she said, punctuating her statement with a bite of cotton candy.

He stared at her for so long she grew uncomfortable and wiped at imaginary pink sugar on her face. "What?" she finally asked.

"You just surprised me, that's all. For someone who wants fame, you just turned down the chance for an autograph and photo op with fans.

She shrugged. "I think that would be obvious. I love to sing. I want to be recognized for my voice. It's about the music, not being identified everywhere I go or losing my anonymity." She blushed as she said, "I'm really shy at heart."

"I love that about you," he said, his eyes softening

as he spoke. "Promise me something?"

She ran her tongue over her bottom lip. "What?" she asked softly.

"Whatever happens in the future, don't change." He leaned closer, his lips hovering over hers. "Don't lose that innate sweetness inside of you, okay?"

"Okay." She couldn't imagine being anything or anyone other than what or who she was.

Her eyes fluttered closed, and his lips touched hers, so gently it brought tears to her eyes. He prolonged the kiss, but it didn't grow hot, heavy, or hungry. Instead it was an honest, genuine expression of feelings. Feelings he held inside and didn't express with words.

Emotions she felt building and growing inside her every day and wished she could set free, but she refrained. Given the constraints of the time they had together and the earlier promises she'd made, it was better to hold the words close to her heart.

"Hey, how about I win you that stuffed animal you wanted?" he offered.

She grinned and placed her hand in his, determined to focus on the here and now. Not the uncertain future.

BEN DROVE THEM home an hour later, a huge stuffed

animal in the back seat. He was uncharacteristically relaxed, having enjoyed today more than any in recent memory. They ordered in dinner and passed out early, only to be awakened by the incessant buzzing of a phone. His sat quietly on the nightstand.

Yawning, Summer reached for hers. "It's Anna. She's texting me," she murmured. "Something about me is blowing up on social media." She opened her phone and began to scroll through Instagram. "Oh, wow. Ummm... Yeah."

"What?" he asked, nerves suddenly awake and aware.

She glanced up at him with a hesitant expression. "I'm not sure you're going to like this."

He pushed himself back against the headboard. "What is it?"

"A photo ... actually a video of us at the carnival went viral. And we're not just kissing." She wrinkled her nose and turned the phone his way.

His eyes opened wide as he watched himself lick cotton candy off her finger in what looked like a very seductive act. Even watching it caused his dick to harden as the memory of the moment came back to him, his tongue wound around her finger, wishing he could take it further and suck at her nipples, visibly tight beneath her shirt.

He muttered a curse as humiliation and frustration

filled him at being caught out in public. "Fuck."

She turned toward him, sitting up in the bed. "I'm sorry. I know this is the last thing you need. I can talk to Dan myself if you want…"

"It's fine." It was actually embarrassing as hell, but hopefully he'd live it down and it wouldn't affect him professionally.

He didn't think Dan would be pissed, and Ben's position at Alpha Security was secure. Dan was more understanding than hard-ass when it came to his people. They'd had the conversation when he hired Ben on and spoke about his past, but would clients care?

"My name isn't mentioned, is it?" he asked, shoulders tight.

"No," she murmured. "At least not yet."

"What does that mean?"

"Well…" she said hesitantly. "I was thinking that if Tawny wanted to get involved and stir up trouble for us, she could possibly post who the mystery man in the video is. Because that's who you are right now. My mystery man."

He winced, really not wanting to be outed by name in Tawny's search for success.

"I'm sorry. I know it's a low point of being with me," Summer murmured, her gaze and expression sad. "If you'd kept your distance like you wanted to in the beginning, this wouldn't have happened."

And he wouldn't have had such a great day with her, nor would he have memories built and stored away. Did he like the fact that they'd been caught? No. He prized anonymity, and he deliberately didn't have a social media profile. But he'd known who she was when he'd gotten involved, even if he hadn't thought through this kind of consequence.

SHE SPENT THE morning liking messages, talking to fans she hadn't known she had, and thanking well-wishers who wanted her to win the position as open-ing act. Ben watched her cheeks flush and her anticipation build as she realized people wanted her to win this competition and open for a major pop star.

She'd finally pulled herself out of bed and was go-ing to shower when her doorbell rang. It had been awhile since she'd had company other than Ivy, and Ben beat her to the door.

"Who is it?" he asked. Although things had been quiet since the attempted drugging, he wouldn't let down his guard.

"Summer? Who is that?" a female voice called from the hall. "Ira, I think it's a man," he heard the woman say.

"Oh my God. It's my mom!" Summer grabbed for

the handle.

"Summer?" a male voice joined in from outside.

"And my dad!" She pulled open the door. "I didn't know you were in town!" Ushering them in, she grabbed first her mother, then her father in a hug. "I'm so glad to see you!"

"Who is this?" Her father glared up at Ben, who was, for him, an unfamiliar man in his daughter's apartment.

"Ben Hollander," Ben said, extending his hand. Despite his having worked on *Star Power*, having been on the set, and having slept with Summer, he'd never officially met them.

"Ben is my bodyguard," Summer said, explaining his presence in her apartment. Something Ben thought they ought to already know, and would have if they'd showed any interest in Summer at all.

"Bodyguard? Why would you need a bodyguard?" Ira, a tall man with gray hair, asked as he shook Ben's hand.

"That's a long story," Summer said. "But basically it's a precaution. Something Jade Glow's people put in place for both me and Tawny." She shot Ben a look, which he interpreted to mean not to give them details about the specifics of someone wanting to hurt her.

"Come in!" She settled her parents on the sofa. "Can I get you anything?"

Her mother shook her head. "We wanted to talk to you." She shot a glance at Ben.

He took the hint that they wanted privacy for their conversation. "I can make myself scarce." He'd go to the bedroom or the kitchen.

In this small apartment, he'd hear everything, but he wasn't leaving her unprotected. Anyone watching would know he left the building and see opportunity.

He was staying put.

★　★　★

SUMMER DIDN'T KNOW what to make of her parents' visit, but she was glad they were here. So much had happened lately that she'd normally talk to her mother about, and she hoped today meant they could make inroads toward regaining their once close relationship.

She glanced at her folks. Her mom looked as fit in person as she had on the video chat, wearing a striped dress with a belt and ballet flats. Her dad, too, was tanned and healthy.

"So, you two look great," Summer said as an ice-breaker.

"Thank you. So do you." Her mom met her gaze, the same golden-brown eyes Summer saw in the mirror staring back at her.

Her mother squirmed in her seat. "Honey, I know when I came back I was still on a high from exploring the world, but really, when I think about that conversation, I just cringe."

Before Summer could reply, her mother rushed on.

"We had our neighbors DVR your *Morning Show* appearance and your whole childhood came rushing back." She sniffed and wiped a tear. "I'm so proud of you. You could have fallen apart or walked off the stage, but my God, you stepped up." Her voice cracked with feeling. "I couldn't imagine what you were going through, alone there, dealing with things."

Summer's eyes glazed, emotion clogging her throat. "I wasn't alone. I had…" She'd been about to say Ben, but then she'd have to explain to her parents that she was sleeping with her bodyguard while he was no doubt listening from the other room. "I was okay," she said over the lump in her throat. "But I did wish you were there. Or at least watching."

Her father nodded. "That's why we're here. Seeing the performance was a wakeup call to how selfish we've been, only thinking about our feelings and not yours. We were hurt," he said. "And angry that after all we'd done to help you get to where you were, you didn't think we are good enough to keep around."

Summer shook her head. She'd never wanted them to feel that way. "That wasn't it. Honestly. It really came down to experience in how to negotiate with people who've been in the industry for years." She'd tried to explain the situation at the time, but they'd been too hurt to hear. "You were great when I was younger, but things got so crazy during and after *Star Power*, and I needed qualified people in my corner. But I never wanted you to all but disappear."

"That was mostly my fault," her father said in a gruff tone. "My ego took a hit, and I decided if you didn't want us managing your career, then you could handle things on your own."

"It was petty and juvenile," her mother said, eyes still watering.

Summer no longer cared about what they'd done or why. She was just grateful they'd had an epiphany. She'd really missed having her parents in her life in any meaningful way. "I'm just happy you're here now."

Her mother pulled her into a hug, and her father followed. Her parents' loving, strong arms reassuring her she had them in her corner.

"Now what's this about a bodyguard?" her father asked. "I wish I'd known about it. You could have told us." He attempted to scold her, but she wasn't going to let him.

"No, I couldn't have." She pursed her lips, waving a chiding finger at him. "And you know now." Time for a change of subject, she thought. "Want to stay for lunch?"

"We'd love to, but we have show tickets for later

today. How about tomorrow? We're here for a few days, and we hope you'll make time for us."

"You know I will." She was fine with them not being able to stay. She'd gotten all she could have wanted from them today anyway. "I'll walk you out."

Ben was out of the kitchen in an instant, taking the lead and opening the door. "Nice to meet you," he said, holding the door open as her father left first.

"Take care of my little girl," Ira said in a protective tone.

Ben inclined his head. "Count on it."

"He's hot," her mother leaned down and whispered in her ear.

Summer couldn't help but laugh. And for the first time in a long time, everything felt right.

Chapter Eleven

B EN READ OVER the plan for the media junket for
Jade Glow's album and upcoming tour, located at
an upscale hotel in Midtown Manhattan. For Summer,
the event, scheduled to last one day, would include
portrait sessions, TV and radio interviews, and
roundtable conversations with Summer, Tawny, and of
course, the star herself.

This go-round, Ben planned to meet up with security and make sure he was satisfied with the situation,
the cameras, and the coverage. Although Ben would
keep Summer in sight, he'd be damned happy when
she wasn't prancing around in front of media and
strangers, at least until whoever was after her had
finally been found.

From a rational protection perspective, he'd also
be glad when the decision was finally made about who
would be the person accompanying Jade Glow on her
world tour. But Ben wasn't feeling particularly rational,

because a part of him didn't want this situation to come to an end. Despite all his internal warnings to himself, he was invested in Summer on every level, and losing her wasn't something he'd ever be ready to think about.

Jade hadn't decided definitely when she would be announcing her choice, but she'd been teasing the possibility that it would happen tonight, at the end of the junket. The star was using the mystery angle on social media for the last few days as well as teasing reporters all day, reminding them to stay until the end, lest they miss her possible announcement. Even Ben had bought into the hype, his stomach in complete knots, thinking his time with Summer was almost over. For her part, Summer was jumpy and nervous, to the point where he didn't know what to say to calm her, her sole focus on the upcoming decision.

During the first hour of chats, she'd been stiff with the interviewers, which wasn't like her. She was normally bubbly, happy, and relaxed, but Jade's teasing and the unknown time frame had her nerves shot. The one thing Ben knew for sure was that he wanted her to live her dream, and to do that, she needed to relax and have a smile on her face and an easy answer on her sexy lips.

They had a good chunk of time before her next set of interviews, and the good news was that she had a hotel suite to escape to between sessions. And he knew just how to calm her frazzled nerves.

★ ★ ★

SUMMER HAD JUST finished up an interview that didn't go as well as she would have liked. Tawny was upbeat, interrupting so she had center stage, and throwing Summer off her game. Frustrated afterwards, she walked off, heading for the coffee stand in the far corner of the event floor.

Before she reached her destination, Ben, who was never out of her sight, stopped her. "Come on," he said, grasping her elbow. "I'm taking you upstairs to chill out."

"But I need caffeine."

He shook his head in definite disagreement. "Caffeine is the last thing you should be putting in your body. Trust me, princess, I have the solution."

"But—"

"No buts. You need a break and you've got free time," he insisted, directing her to the bank of elevators leading to the suite they'd been given as a courtesy for the day.

"Fine. Let's go up," she said in a tense tone. She didn't mean to be a bitch, but she was upset with how today was going. She didn't want the opportunity to slip by her because Tawny knew how to get the first and last word.

The elevator doors opened, and Ben placed a hand on her back, stepping out into the hall and guiding her to the room at the far end, where earlier they'd dropped off her cosmetics and a change of clothes, just in case.

He slid the key card over the sensor, and the green light flashed. He opened the door, propping it with one foot so she could step inside.

No sooner had she entered than Ben swung her into his arms. "Ben!" She grabbed him around his neck so she could hold on. "What are you doing?"

"I'm going to relax you."

"How?"

He grinned and strode to the big king-size bed, depositing her in the center. "How do you think?" He slid his wallet from his jeans, removed a condom, and dropped it onto the bed.

"Ooh," she said, completely on board with his notion of relaxation.

He grasped her legs, sliding her down toward where he stood at the edge of the mattress. Her skirt rode up, revealing her barely there thong panties, which he promptly removed. Cool air rushed over her suddenly damp flesh, causing her hips to wriggle, need flushing across her skin.

His gaze narrowed on her swollen sex.

Aroused, she slid her legs farther apart in readiness, absolutely on board with his plan.

She didn't want to worry until the next round of interviews. Leave it to Ben to take care of her. "I like the way you think."

"I realize you have to be back downstairs and need time to pull yourself together after." He dropped his holster onto the floor, unbuttoned his jeans, his cock springing free, hard and thick. "Ready for a fast ride?"

She ran her tongue over her lips, her gaze on his pulsing erection. "I'm ready for you."

He bent his head and swirled his tongue around her already needy sex. She groaned and grasped on to the bedding as he ate at her like a man who couldn't get enough, who had single-minded focus, and whose attention was wholly centered on her. After all their time together, he knew what she liked and needed and immediately zeroed in on her clit.

Desire slammed into her hard and fast, no slow buildup, just zero to sixty, her climax suddenly and quickly within reach. She moaned and switched her grasp from the bedspread to his hair, holding him in place while she rocked her face against his mouth, chasing the waves of pleasure that rushed through her.

He tongued her clit in a perfect rhythm that had her spiraling higher until she peaked, her orgasm taking her into utter bliss. She was lost to sensation, only coming back to herself when Ben, sheathed with a condom, settled between her thighs.

The head of his cock breached her entrance, but she had no time to focus. His mouth came down on hers, and she tasted her musky scent on his lips. At the same moment, he took her hard, his erection thrusting into her.

"F-u-c-k," he said, drawing out the syllable. He dropped down over her, bracing his hands on either side of her shoulders, his chest reverberating against hers.

"Ben, God." She felt him everywhere as he throbbed inside her, her inner walls clasping him tight, her emotions fully engaged as their bodies joined completely.

Instead of a hard and fast taking, Ben rocked into her, grinding against her clit with every shift and pitch of his hips. Sensation began to take hold and build once more. Swirling need enveloped her, and she cried out, the sweet feelings he inspired driving her higher and higher.

"Come with me," he said, sliding a hand between their bodies and pressing against her most sensitive spot.

"Oh God." Waves of desire shook her, sparks of pleasure shooting out from her clit to every nerve ending she possessed. "Ben. I'm coming!"

"Right there with you," he promised and he began a punishing rhythm. She exploded once more, her climax a burst of glorious light and feeling, as he groaned and came, too, her name on his lips.

He collapsed on top of her, and they panted in unison, until reality slowly returned.

"Can't breathe," she said, and he rolled off her, keeping her hand in his as he fell onto his back.

"That was a real stress reducer." She grinned, but inside she was more serious than she'd ever been. Because what had just happened between them?

That was too intense to soothe her. Instead all she could do was feel—Ben inside her, Ben coaxing her to come, calling her name as he climaxed right after her. The sensations went beyond sex. He had tagged every emotion she had: Love, caring, yearning.

Things she would need time to process and deal with. Things she had to find a place for in her life … once she knew what her future held. She felt pulled in two different directions, her love for Ben and the career she'd been working toward her entire life, causing a quiet and somber blanket of emotion to envelop her. She wanted to give Ben the time he deserved, and she didn't have that ability now.

"I need to wash up," she said, sitting up in bed, eager to put the intensity behind them as fast as possible so she could prepare for the rest of the day.

"Come." He rose and walked to the bathroom, his bare ass peeking from beneath his shirt.

The man had a body to die for and drool over and a heart that was bigger than he'd like to admit. And she wished they could spend more time alone here, in bed. Talking. Figuring out *them*. But she needed her focus where it belonged, on the media downstairs and the probable announcement coming later tonight.

So she pushed herself to a standing position and went to get ready to return to the press junket downstairs.

★ ★ ★

HOURS LATER, SUMMER felt like she was ready to collapse in exhaustion. Her last interview had just ended. There wasn't a reporter she hadn't spoken to or a question she hadn't answered. But she had to admit her romp with Ben had given her the emotional boost she'd needed to push through the rest of the day.

Every time she'd looked up, he'd been there, not just watching over her as part of his job but playing the part of passionate supporter. A thumbs-up, a wink, a smile had all let her know he was there, in her corner, paying attention. She didn't think she could love him more.

What to do about that love?

"What's your plan?" he asked her, joining her and

interrupting her thoughts.

"Jade said to be back downstairs at eight. I thought I'd lie down for an hour. I'm wiped out."

Sympathy flashed in his expression. "Let's get you to bed."

Memories of their earlier time upstairs flashed through her mind, him making love to her—and she refused to think they'd shared anything less—his big body filling hers, causing her to tremble.

He met her gaze, a knowing grin on his handsome face. "No, princess. Not for that. You need to rest this time."

She pretended to pout and he laughed.

"Come on." Ben escorted her upstairs and literally tucked her into bed.

She set her phone alarm just in case she fell asleep, and placed it on the nightstand.

"All set?" he asked.

She nodded.

"Good." He braced a hand above her head, leaned down, and kissed her softly on the lips, lingering … and she thought maybe he'd be crawling in beside her, but his phone rang.

He pulled his cell out and answered. "Hollander." He listened and nodded. "I'll be right there." He disconnected the call. "That was someone on Jade's security detail. They want to give me a quick recon of the area Jade requested for her press conference. Since I've been all over them about details, I guess they're being proactive. Can't say I'm complaining. Though I've been pleased with how they've handled things so far."

Summer smiled at his professional tone. "Jade's not going to take her own safety for granted."

"And I'm not going to take yours," he said, dead serious.

She hooked her arms around his neck. "I always feel safe when you're around."

"Good. I'll be back in a few minutes."

"Okay." She closed her eyes and heard the hotel room door slam shut behind him.

She sighed, allowing her body to relax and meld into the mattress. She refused to think ahead to tonight's decision. Jade, in calling for the special gathering after the junket, had obviously decided to announce her choice in opening act. Despite her flipping stomach, nerves, and anticipation, for now, all Summer wanted to do was just *be*.

She was so relaxed beneath the covers that she almost didn't hear the knock on her room door until it became a persistent banging that interrupted her tranquility. Ben had a key card, so she kept her eyes closed, hoping whoever it was would go away.

When the noise didn't stop, she shoved the heavenly covers off herself and padded in her bare feet to the door, glancing into the peephole, finding Michael there.

She frowned. Anna, she knew, would be here tonight, now that the decision was imminent, but until she arrived, Michael might have information Summer needed.

Still annoyed at the interruption of her rest, she opened the door and leaned on the frame, not letting him into her private space.

"Summer! What took you so long?" he asked, sounding frantic.

"I was resting. What's wrong?"

"Jade. Jade wants to meet with you and Tawny before her announcement tonight. I'm assuming she's going to tell you her choice before the rest of the world. I need you to come with me."

Summer's stomach flipped in excitement. "Where is Tawny?"

"She's already downstairs. Come on. Let's go!" He moved in closer, but she didn't open her door for him to step through.

"Ben's not back yet," she said. "I can't just leave."

"Do you want to blow your possible chances? The bodyguard will understand. You're with your agent. Well, closest thing to your agent until Anna shows up later. Now move it!"

She jumped into action. "Let me grab my shoes." She shut the door in his face and slipped back into her high heels, rushing back to meet Michael in the hallway, where he continued to pace back and forth, his nerves worse than her own. "I'm ready."

"It's about time," he muttered, grasping her elbow and turning the opposite direction from the bank of elevators.

"Where are you going?" She tugged her arm out of his grasp.

"The paparazzi are all over downstairs, waiting for a glimpse of Jade or you and Tawny. I've been using the service elevator. It's safer."

Summer frowned but she agreed, having been through the crush of photographers and reporters earlier. He held on to her arm, walking her to the far end of the hall and the single elevator there. A house-keeper joined them, waiting for the lift, which seemed to take forever. Probably because many people had the same idea to avoid the press in the lobby.

Michael was practically hopping from foot to foot, his nerves driving her crazy.

"I can't believe I'm telling *you* to relax," she said, taking in the irony. It was her life about to change, one way or another.

"It's a huge day," he muttered, staring at the housekeeper's back. "Let's just take the stairs."

"What?"

He pulled her by the arm, and she teetered on her heels before righting herself. "Michael, chill out! We'll get there." She followed him across the hall, into the stairwell, and down a flight of steps.

Her feet hurt and her ankles wobbled in the too high heels.

"Michael, let's just go wait for the service elevator. I can't do stairs in these shoes.

He held on to her tightly. "No. Here's fine."

"What are you doing! Let go of me!"

"We're alone now and we need to talk," he said. "I need your help. You have to do something for me and I'll pay you well." He was talking fast, rambling.

"What is it?" she asked, nervous because he was in her personal space, his big fingers digging into her bare forearms.

"Drop out of the competition. I'll pay you a hundred grand. Just say you're overwhelmed and it's too much for you so you're giving it up to Tawny. Use the money to rent a studio. Go indie. Do something, anything with the cash," he said, shooting out ideas in an obvious panic.

She looked into his wild eyes and saw real desperation, which, along with his hold on her arm and her proximity to the edge of the stairs in her ridiculously high heels, scared her. "What's this about?" she asked quietly, hoping to calm him.

"My life. Life as I know it. Tawny's threatening to tell my wife about our affair if I don't secure her this opportunity. I have a prenup. Cheating means I get nothing. *Nothing!*" he shouted at her.

He was sleeping with Tawny? And she was black-mailing him? "Michael, were you behind everything that's happened to me? The trashing of my dressing room, attempting to drug me?"

Regret flashed in his eyes. "I had no choice. You didn't take any hint. When you performed on *The Morning Show*, you should have bombed and slipped away in disgrace. Instead you pulled out a win." He ran a shaking hand through his hair. "You didn't scare off after I warned you to drop out. I thought if you took that drink you'd get so sexually aggressive with your bodyguard I could film you and it'd go viral. I never thought he'd be one step ahead of me. I have no choice. Please. Take the money," he all but begged her.

She should have been shocked, but hadn't Ben had a bad feeling about him? But she couldn't just walk away from Jade's competition. She'd invested her entire life to have this one chance at stardom.

She glanced at Michael, who watched her anxiously.

"I can't," she said. "Don't you see? This opportunity is everything to me. Maybe if you talk to your wife, apologize…"

"Shut up! Just be quiet. I can't lose everything. My kids. The money. My reputation." He punctuated every word with a near violent shake. Her heel slipped and she nearly fell down the stairs. Only his grasp kept her upright.

Her heart pounded hard in her chest, real fear taking hold. He wasn't at all rational in his panic. Jade's deadline had made him crazy.

"All you need to do is say you changed your mind. Say you can't handle the pressure of opening for such a big star." He repeated his earlier words. "And I'll wire money into your account today." He pulled his phone from his pocket, never releasing his grip on her with his other hand. "Here. I'll record." He held up the video camera on his phone.

"Michael, this is ridiculous. No one will believe—"

"Say it!" he shouted, shaking her hard as he punched a button on his phone and turned the camera to face her.

She didn't want to tumble headfirst down the stairs in her designer heels courtesy of a clearly unhinged man. So when his fingers pinched her skin, she spoke, repeating words she never thought she'd say.

To her shock, after getting what he wanted, Michael released her arm and took off downstairs, running to the press to release the video and ruin her life.

★　★　★

BEN RETURNED TO Summer's room pissed off. He'd gone downstairs only to be told that no one on the security detail had called him for a walk-through. They didn't know what he was talking about, and Ben hated wasting his time. The more he thought about the fake call, the warier he became, and he picked up his pace, rushing back to Summer.

He let himself into the room. In case she was sleeping, he didn't call out, but he headed straight back to the bedroom, where he'd left her a few minutes earlier.

The bed was rumpled … and empty.

"Summer!" He called out her name but already knew she wouldn't answer. Someone had distracted him long enough to lure her away.

He pulled out his phone. No calls from her. No messages.

He dialed her number, but her phone rang uselessly on the nightstand, where she'd left the device earlier.

"Fuck." He strode out through the suite and into the hallway, glancing in either direction, seeing no one.

Suddenly the exit door burst open, and Summer ran into the hall, tripping on her heels. She caught sight of him immediately.

"Ben!" She kicked off her heels so she could run to him.

He caught her in his arms, taking a needed few seconds to hold her tight, breathe in her scent, and know she was safe.

"What the hell happened?" he asked, pulling her back, his gaze taking her in to make sure she was visibly okay.

She gestured to the stairwell with shaking hands. "You were right. It was Michael. He came to my room and said Jade wanted an immediate meeting with me and Tawny," she explained in a rush. "He said Tawny was already there and I needed to hurry. I rushed out with him and forgot my phone."

He swallowed over his urge to yell at her because he knew Michael had chosen the one thing that would coax her out of the safety of her room. "What did he really want?"

"You won't believe this, but he's sleeping with Tawny, and she threatened to tell his wife about their affair if he didn't secure her the opening act. He's been behind everything that's happened because his wife has a prenup and he's afraid of losing everything." She swallowed hard. "He offered me a fortune to drop out, and when I said no, he started shaking me on the stairs, and I was in these heels and petrified I'd go flying down. I mean he's totally crazy. He made me say

I was dropping out on a video recording, and he's downstairs right now playing it for the media."

Ben glanced at her stilettos and groaned, imagining her toppling down headfirst. "That stupid fuck. All you have to do is go down there and explain why you said those things." And he'd get the cops to arrest Gold as soon as possible.

Summer shook her head. "I told you he's insane. He's not thinking clearly or else he'd know that."

"But you're okay? He didn't hurt you?" he asked, hating that she'd been alone with him, even for a short amount of time.

"I'm fine."

He inclined his head, forcing himself to breathe calmly and believe her. "Then let's go fix this mess."

He pulled out his phone and hit the stored number he had for Jade Glow's security, quickly relaying what he knew about Michael Gold. "Coming down now," Ben said and shoved his phone into his pocket. "Come on." He grabbed her hand and led her to the main set of elevators. "You need to recant that video."

She bit down on her lower lip. "I hope you're right. And what about Tawny? She was blackmailing him!"

"We'll get it sorted." He met her gaze and tucked a strand of hair behind her ear, hoping to reassure her.

She retrieved her shoes and they waited until the

elevator doors opened. They stepped onto the level where the press junket had taken place. Photographers and reporters were gathered in a group, lights flashing, as they surrounded someone Ben assumed was Michael.

"Come on. Let's sneak up on him." They started to walk around the group of people when a voice called out.

"It's her!" All eyes turned back, finding Summer, and the crowd started toward her.

Ben kept a firm lock on her waist, standing by her side as she was surrounded by reporters.

"Summer!"

"Summer! Is it true? You dropped out? You're handing the opening act to Tawny Renee?"

She squeezed Ben's hand and released it, then drew a deep breath and spoke. "What's true is that I made that tape under duress. Michael Gold, Tawny's agent, lured me to a solitary stairwell and offered me a huge amount of money to drop out, and when I refused, he nearly pushed me down the stairs while demanding I make that video."

"Liar!" Michael lunged forward but security grabbed him, holding him in place.

The crowd erupted, shouting more questions, the predominant one being why Michael would go to those extremes.

Summer glanced at Ben, and he gave her a subtle nod, encouraging her to tell everything to the press.

"Mr. Gold is having an affair with Tawny Renee. According to him, she was blackmailing him, threatening to tell his wife about the affair unless he did whatever he had to in order to get me to drop out of the competition. I've been the victim of quite a few incidents, including an attempted drugging—all documented by the police."

"You lying bitch!" Michael would have gone after her if two men weren't already holding him tight, but Summer eased closer to Ben.

"She's not lying." Tawny pushed through the throng of reporters and faced Michael. "You had one job and you couldn't do it right. I didn't ask you to hurt her; I just asked you to get me this position."

"You threatened to reveal everything to my wife! What did you think I'd do?" Michael shouted back.

"Do they not realize they have an audience?" Summer whispered to Ben as reporters captured every word between them, as did the police, who'd arrived and surrounded Michael and the security holding him.

"Let me go!"

"We're bringing you down for questioning. You, too, Ms. Renee."

Tawny appeared horrified. "What? No. I had nothing to do with this crazy scheme of his!"

"From what I understand, Mr. Gold is being accused of false imprisonment, he's accused you of blackmailing him, and according to police reports on file, we have numerous other offenses that potentially involve you both. So you can come willingly or we can do this the hard way." The officer pulled out handcuffs, giving Tawny a choice as to how she wanted to proceed.

"Fine. I'll come. But you're going to realize I'm innocent. And I want my lawyer," she said, stomping off with the officer in charge.

Michael was already being taken away by the police, photographers and reporters documenting the entire humiliating thing.

Summer turned to Ben, looking up at him, gratitude and what he wanted to believe was something more in her eyes. "Thank you. I don't know how I would have gotten through this without you by my side."

He didn't want to say he was just doing his job, because although that's how this had begun, it was by no means how it was ending.

She placed her hand in his. "I don't know what's going to happen next but—"

"Summer!" At the sound of her name, Summer turned.

Ben glanced over to see Jade Glow approach, surrounded by security of her own. With her long, flowing red hair, green eyes, and heavily done makeup, she stood out in any crowd. But once she drew closer, Ben realized she looked younger than the persona she liked to project to the world.

"Summer, I can't believe everything I just heard! I'm so sorry I set you up for a competition that led to something like this," the pop star said. "Let's talk."

Summer shot Ben a regret-filled glance. He understood she felt pulled in two directions, wanting to finish her conversation with him and needing to see what Jade wanted to discuss.

Knowing what he had to do, for her sake, he stepped back and let Jade take Summer's attention. Summer's agent joined them soon after. Summer kept glancing over her shoulder to see if he was there, guilt and worry in her expression. He couldn't have that. As much as Ben wanted to wait around, all that would accomplish was pulling Summer's concentration away from where it needed to be.

He headed up to her room to wait, but after an hour, he realized she wasn't coming back anytime soon. He had his duffel with all his things because he packed light and they'd talked about staying over depending on how late today's event ran. If he walked out of here now, he had no reason to go back to her place except to talk. And he didn't know if or even when she'd arrive there, tonight or tomorrow.

And she no longer needed a bodyguard, which meant he had no choice but to go home.

Chapter Twelve

SUMMER APPRECIATED THE fact that she'd be opening for Jade, although she would have liked to have achieved her goal with a lot less angst and drama. At first she'd kept looking over at Ben, hoping to convey that she hated that she'd had to cut their conversation short. She didn't even know what, exactly, she wanted to say to him, but she wasn't ready to lose him just because his assignment had come to an abrupt end.

When she glanced over again and realized he had left, her stomach pitched in disappointment and frustration. Still, she had no choice but to devote all her energy and focus on Jade. They made their way to the star's private suite, which was a massive set of rooms, punctuated by a large living area filled with flowers and a baby grand piano as the centerpiece.

Jade had been set to choose Summer, anyway, and she went on to explain that in addition to her own personal preference, that Ourstage.com, an site that allowed fans to choose their favorite act, had skewed heavily for Summer, as well.

The rest of the evening passed in a blur of conversation and planning among Summer, Jade, and their agents, and a lavish meal ordered by Jade, and by the time Summer returned to her room, she was ready to pass out from exhaustion. Her adrenaline rush was gone, and when she entered the empty room, she realized immediately that so was Ben.

Over the course of the evening, she hadn't had time to even look at her phone. Now that she did, she saw that Ben had left her a text.

You deserve every bit of this success. Go live your dream. Love, Ben.

She reread his closing words, *Love, Ben*, trying to decide whether or not to read more into it than mere words. And even if he meant them in the truest sense, did it change anything? She'd achieved her biggest dream, and yet she was alone in a Midtown hotel room.

He hadn't waited around and she didn't blame him. If she had no time for him after today's mess of events, how would she have time when she left on a world tour? She didn't see any way to make a relationship between them work that was fair to Ben. And it was that thought that kept her from going after him.

★   ★   ★

BEN RETURNED TO the office, feeling out of sorts. A weekend alone in his apartment did nothing to improve the mood he'd been in since leaving Summer behind.

He walked into the main area, where Tara Hayes, the receptionist for Alpha Security, sat at her desk. Tara was in her mid-forties, an attractive woman who always dressed appropriately regardless of everyone else being office casual. Today her hair was pulled into a bun, and she dressed in a white buttoned-up top and a black skirt.

"Good morning," she said, a smile on her face.

"Morning. Everything good?" he asked, trying his best to be cheerful and not punish the world because he was miserable.

"Things are running like clockwork around here, which makes me happy, as you know."

Ben nodded, knowing Tara kept Dan organized and the office running smoothly. "You're Dan's right hand. We all appreciate everything you do."

"Aww, thank you." She blushed at the compliment. "I like to feel part of the team."

"Ben! My office. Now." Dan stood outside his door and gestured for Ben to join him.

"The boss bellows," Tara said, laughing.

Ben went around Tara's desk and strode into

Dan's office. His boss had sat back down in his oversized chair. "I thought you could use a debrief." Dan eyed him with concern. "In other words, I want to know if you're okay. I caught the entertainment news this weekend."

"Yeah, so did I," Ben muttered.

Although he wasn't normally a gossip show watcher, the masochist in him had put on nightly shows anyway, hoping to see how they were covering Jade Glow and her new opening act. He'd seen full treatments on Michael Gold's arrest, Tawny's questioning by the police, and of course, Jade's official announcement choosing Summer as her opening act.

Summer glowed, standing beside Jade, exuding pride and excitement, and he couldn't be happier for her.

Even if it meant he'd lost her.

"You let her go?" Dan asked.

"What was I supposed to do? Ask her to put her dreams on hold?" Not that he hadn't been tempted. He just wasn't that much of an asshole.

Dan shook his head, spinning a pen between his palms. "I know I didn't raise you, but I still like to think I had enough time with you to instill a few things in that thick skull of yours."

Ben swallowed hard. "I know you lost Katherine," he said of Dan's wife. "But—"

"But nothing. Life is too fucking short. You grab on to happiness while you can. Isn't that what I try to teach all of you?"

"I understand where you're coming from, and I respect it, but really, she's worked her whole life for this opportunity."

Dan rolled his eyes. "I'm not suggesting you ask her to give it up. Let me ask you something. What do you do for a living?" He folded his arms across his chest and eyed Ben through narrowed lids.

Ben tipped his head. "I'm a bodyguard, obviously." What the fuck was the man getting at? Ben wondered.

"And what does a pop star need when she travels? A full-time bodyguard," Dan spelled out for him, a grin on his face.

"Son of a bitch," Ben muttered, the solution so simple he was shocked he hadn't figured it out for himself. He glanced at his boss, awe and admiration filling him. "You're willing to lose me?"

"Well, hell, son. I received a call from the company that hired us in the first place. They want to keep you on as Summer's security detail. It seems Jade Glow took a liking to your girl and wants to keep her safe."

Ben blinked in surprise.

"I'd call that a win-win, for you and for Alpha Security," he said somewhat smugly. "Works for me. Can I tell them you accept the job?"

"Of course," Ben said, his head spinning at the one-eighty he'd done since walking into this office. He only wanted Summer to be happy and follow her dream, never thinking he could be part of it.

Ben walked toward Dan, who rose from his seat. "I don't know how to thank you for getting my head on straight," he said to the man who, in the short time he'd worked for him, was often more like a father than his own parent had been.

Dan placed an arm around his shoulders. "Nothing gives me greater pleasure than seeing all of you happy. I just wish the others would follow suit."

Who'd have thought Dan was a matchmaker at heart? "You know I wish the same for you." Ben patted Dan on the back.

Dan met his gaze, his expression serious and sad. "I had my time. It ended too soon, but I couldn't ask for better than the life I had with Katherine." His eyes glazed at the memory of the wife he loved so much. "That's why I'm willing to let one of my best men take a job that will send him to the other side of the world for half the year. Because you love that girl. I could tell by watching you two together."

Ben thought back to the time he'd brought Summer to Dan's house for his birthday. "That was very early in our relationship."

Which, he knew, had formed within the bubble of

both a condensed time frame and close living quarters. But he didn't think that lessened what they felt for each other, but heightened their emotions instead. He loved her, probably had for a lot longer than he'd wanted to admit. He'd been fighting his past and himself.

"I'm pretty schooled in reading people. Now are you going to go get your girl?" Dan asked.

"Hell yes." Ben was planning to offer her everything he had. Which wasn't much considering where she was headed in her career, but he was discovering that he was a romantic at heart.

He loved her. Everything else would fall into place. He'd accept nothing less, he thought, his anticipation heightened at the thought of being with Summer with no barriers between them, and his heart on the line.

HAVING ACHIEVED HER dream, Summer should be on top of the world. Instead she was sitting with a tub of cookie dough ice cream in front of her, a glass of white wine on the table beside her, and her best friend, who'd dropped everything to commiserate with her, sitting across the way.

She dug into the creamy dessert and savored the cookie crunch. "I promised myself this one night to mourn what might have been, and then I'm throwing myself into getting ready for the tour. No tears after tonight." She placed the ice cream down on the table and lifted the glass of wine. "To the man I love and can't have."

Ivy shook her head, clearly not happy with how Summer was handling her life. "Honey, if you love him, you need to tell him."

Summer bit down on her lower lip. "I would but telling him isn't fair to him. What would I say? I love you but I'm leaving anyway? See you in six months? Or longer?"

"Exactly," Ivy said on a nod. "If he loves you, he'll wait." She took a sip of her wine, then asked, "Does he? Love you, I mean?"

Their past flashed before her eyes. The laughter, the fun at the carnival, the sensual looks... And at the end, there was that text... *Love, Ben,* he'd said. Had that been a generic sign-off? Or a real expression from the heart?

His words when he'd been lost inside her, calling out, *mine. Mine.* She trembled at the memory that had made her feel so cherished, so loved. Just like their last time together, when he'd relaxed her in the hotel room, him buried deep inside her, rocking against her, taking her to completion in such a tender ... and, again, loving way.

"I think he loves me," she whispered. "And I

know for a fact that I love him."

And yet she'd ignored him that last day. Then she hadn't answered his text because she didn't know what to say… Thanks for being my bodyguard? Have a nice life? I'll miss you?

So she'd let the rest of the weekend go by but … *she loved him.* "I need to talk to him. He needs to know how I feel."

Ivy grinned. "See? You didn't need me here at all," she said, laughing. "You just needed a good self-talking-to."

"Where's my phone?" Summer asked as a knock sounded at her door.

"I've got it." Ivy jumped up to see who was there, looking into the peephole. "Oh my God! It's him!"

Summer rose from her seat, running a shaking hand over her ice-cream-stained top "Look at me!"

Her hair was pulled into a messy bun on top of her head. She had no makeup on, and her eyes were puffy from the occasional tears she'd shed over Ben. And her clothes? Not only were they stained but her soft cotton shorts and old tee shirt were threadbare—because she hadn't cared what she wore to wallow over losing Ben.

He pounded on the door again.

"No time to change," Ivy said, laughing but showing her no pity as she unlocked the door and let Ben inside. "Hi, bodyguard," she said.

"Hi, Ivy. Summer here?"

She cleared her throat.

He stepped past Ivy, looking determined and oh so sexy. He met her gaze, his expression softening as he took her in.

"Hi," she whispered. Despite all the heavy emotions flowing through her, most of all certainty about how strongly she loved him, she was suddenly uncertain of how to approach him.

In the wake of the silence as they stared at each other, Ivy gathered her bag from the couch. "And I'll take this as my cue to leave," she said, making her way to the door.

"Bye, Ivy," Summer said, her stare never leaving Ben.

"Text me later. I want details," she said, not ashamed to be blunt.

"Good-bye!" Summer said, shaking her head over her friend.

Ivy closed the door as she left, leaving Summer alone with Ben.

"I wasn't expecting you." She tried not to feel self-conscious about her messy appearance as she gestured for him to come farther inside.

"I couldn't let another minute go by." He strode up to her, grasping her face between his hands and staring into her eyes. "I love you, Summer."

Her heart skipped a beat at his words. "You what?" she asked, blinking up at him. She knew she'd heard him right, but she definitely needed to hear him say it again.

A sweet, sexy smile lifted his lips. "I love you, Summer. Need me to say it again?"

She shook her head, tears of joy filling her eyes and happiness clogging her throat. "I love you, too," she said, but in her heart, she knew their problems weren't solved just because they'd admitted their feelings. "But what about—"

He cut her words off, sealing his lips over hers instead. In his kiss, in the reverent way his mouth moved over hers, his thumb caressing the side of her face, she felt the love he'd expressed in those three simple words that meant so much.

It hadn't been long since she'd seen him last, but she'd missed him, probably more so because she believed their separation was permanent. At the thought, she wound her arms around his neck and pressed into him, needing to get as close as possible. Her breasts crushed against his chest, and she soaked in his purely masculine scent.

He groaned and slid his tongue into her mouth, uniting them as their bodies meshed and their hips ground together. He dropped his hands from her face, his fingers gliding through her hair. He tipped her head, holding her in place while he kissed her sense-less, and she lost herself in everything that was Ben, and all she could think about was the fact that he was here, he loved her, and … she was leaving soon.

She pulled back, leaning her head so she could meet his gaze. "What are we going to do about the long-distance issue? I can't get back here while on tour, and if you're on a case, you definitely can't come to me."

Pain filled her at the thought, but a pleased look danced across his face, giving her hope he'd thought of a solution she hadn't. "What is it?" she asked.

"You're looking at your new full-time bodyguard," he said, grinning. "As in, where you go, I go."

"Really?" Excitement filled her, but then reality took hold. "Ben, I can't afford to pay you full time."

"You have a guardian angel," he said, kissing her lips. "Dan got a call from Jade's people. Apparently, she's decided to take you under her wing. She feels responsible for setting up the competition and putting you in a position where Michael could try and under-mine you. She and her team want your security covered."

She let his news sink in, Jade's generosity and the fact that she and Ben wouldn't be separated after all. "Oh my God! That's incredible. You're coming with me?" She squealed in excitement. "You're really coming with me! It's like all my dreams wrapped up in one huge, lucky, unbelievable package. I don't know how to thank her."

"You'll find a way," he said, a smile on his face. "But you have to know something. Even if the opportunity hadn't come up, after talking to Dan today about life being short and knowing how he lost the love of his life to cancer … I'd have found a way to make it work. To make *us* work."

She bit down on her lower lip to stop its quivering. "I was talking to Ivy before you came in. And I was going to tell you the same thing. I didn't have a solution, but I knew that I loved you." She grasped on to his shoulders. "And I didn't want to lose you."

"And you never will." Love and so much emotion flashed across his handsome face. "You're going to conquer the world, Summer Michelle. And I'm going to be by your side when you do. Because nobody but me is going to guard this body," he said, his hands grazing down her sides, over her breasts, her nipples tightening at the slightest tease of his touch.

"You can start right now." She grasped his hand and pulled him toward the bedroom, her heart light, her spirits high, her sense of gratitude soaring.

She had the career she'd worked so hard for with the man she loved by her side. She couldn't ask for anything more.

Epilogue

THE ARENA REVERBERATED with music, the last song in Summer's opening act in the final performance of a long tour. Austin Rhodes had showed up at Madison Square Garden along with the other bodyguards at Alpha Security, Dan, and Tara, their receptionist, because Ben was a close friend and they wanted to support him. But as the lights flashed and the music pounded through his body, he felt older than his years. As much as he appreciated Summer's talent, concerts weren't his thing.

That's what having a kid did, it aged him, he thought wryly. Although he'd willingly change the painful past that had brought him to this point, he'd never change a thing about the little girl he adored. Bailey was his world. He had no social life, rarely went out unless he was on the job. Tonight Bailey was home with his nanny, giving him the chance to be here for Ben.

Summer's set ended and Austin clapped, whistling his approval along with the rest of the crew. Instead of being able to leave, they then sat through Jade Glow's concert, as well, before finally meeting up with Ben and Summer backstage.

Ben led them to a relatively quiet corner, away from the insanity of Jade and her entourage. He turned to Austin and slapped him on the back. "I know it wasn't easy for you to make it tonight and I'm grateful."

"Wouldn't miss it," he assured his friend. That's what his live-in nanny was for. Watching the munchkin when Austin had to be out.

"Hey, everyone, can I get your attention?" Ben whistled, quieting down his friends. Everyone was still hyped up from the concert.

Summer joined him, slipping beneath his arm. She'd changed from her stage costume into a pair of jeans and a tee shirt and looked up at Ben with complete adoration in her gaze.

Man, that look was enough to bring a man to his knees. Well, Ben, at least. Austin had been through the wringer with his ex-wife, Bailey's mother, and he'd never let a woman wrap him around her finger again. Not that Ben and Summer had that kind of a relationship. There was a mutual respect between them Austin admired. One he hadn't found in his own past marriage, and he'd learned a hard lesson from being used.

"It's good to have you back," Dan said now that Ben had quieted everyone down.

"We're happy to be home and to settle down for a while," Summer said. "A long while, I hope."

Austin understood. Ben had mentioned she'd be doing work in a recording studio she was renting, and Ben wanted to buy a house so they had a home base beyond their small apartments. They were obviously ready to combine their lives.

"Before we all get busy with work and assignments, I wanted you—my friends I consider family—here when I ask Summer a question," Ben said, a grin on his face.

"What?" Summer swung her head around, meeting his gaze.

Even Jade, the huge pop star, had joined them, slipping into the crowd beside Ava.

Ben reached into his pocket and pulled out a ring box.

Summer gasped.

Ava clapped her hands, obviously excited for her friends.

The other guys, Jared, Tate, and even Shane, who was in town, took a step back as if the upcoming engagement was contagious. Only Dan stood close, a satisfied expression on his face. Everyone knew how

Dan felt about happy endings.

Ben dropped to one knee and looked up at the woman he loved. "Summer Michelle, I knew the day I met you that you were something special and you would rock my world. I just didn't realize the ride we'd take together, and I know it's just the beginning. I love you and I want to spend the rest of my life with you." He popped open the box, revealing a nice, large, sparkling ring.

Not even his ex could quibble with the size of that thing, Austin thought.

Summer's eyes grew wide, happy tears falling down her cheeks.

"Will you marry me?" he asked.

"Yes. Yes!" Before he could put the ring on her finger, she'd wrapped her arms around his neck, holding on tight.

And that was why Austin liked Summer as a match for his friend. Her focus was on her man, not the stone.

A round of applause followed, along with congratulations by everyone there. Austin stuck around long enough to give his good wishes to the happy couple in person before heading home to his daughter.

He wished he could say one day he'd find the right woman for him, but he wasn't willing to get burned again. At this point, he had one goal. To be a good father to his daughter … and to stop thinking dirty, sexy thoughts about the woman he'd hired to care for her.

Thank you for reading ROCK ME. I hope you enjoyed Summer and Ben's story! I would appreciate it if you would help others enjoy this book by leaving a review at your preferred e-tailer. Thank you!

UP NEXT: TEMPT ME – A bodyguard and the nanny story – coming January 2018
ORDER TEMPT ME Today

Bodyguard Bad Boys… Sexy, hot and oh so protective!

Burned by an ex with a wandering eye, Austin Rhodes has sworn off women. His sole focus is his young daughter – and despite his good intentions, the little girl's live-in nanny. He hired Mia Atwood to care for his child but he finds himself lusting after her instead. Keeping his distance isn't easy but he's determined to be a gentleman. Until Mia's past comes back to haunt her and she's in need of Austin's brand of protection. Suddenly she's his in every sense of the word—and he'll do whatever it takes to shield the woman who tempts him beyond reason.

Keep up with Carly and her upcoming books:

Website:
www.carlyphillips.com

Sign up for Carly's Newsletter:
www.carlyphillips.com/newsletter-sign-up

Carly on Facebook:
www.facebook.com/CarlyPhillipsFanPage

Carly on Twitter:
www.twitter.com/carlyphillips

Hang out at Carly's Corner! (Hot guys & giveaways!)
smarturl.it/CarlysCornerFB

CARLY'S MONTHLY CONTEST!

Visit: www.carlyphillips.com/newsletter-sign-up and enter for a chance to win the prize of the month! You'll also automatically be added to her newsletter list so you can keep up on the newest releases!

About the Author

Carly Phillips is the *N.Y. Times* and *USA Today* Bestselling Author of over 50 sexy contemporary romance novels featuring hot men, strong women and the emotionally compelling stories her readers have come to expect and love. Carly's career spans over a decade and a half with various New York publishing houses, and she is now an Indie author who runs her own business and loves every exciting minute of her publishing journey. Carly is happily married to her college sweetheart, the mother of two nearly adult daughters and three crazy dogs (two wheaten terriers and one mutant Havanese) who star on her Facebook Fan Page and website. Carly loves social media and is always around to interact with her readers. You can find out more about Carly at www.carlyphillips.com.

Made in the USA
San Bernardino, CA
06 September 2017